HUSBAND POTENTIAL

HUSBAND POTENTIAL

BY

REBECCA WINTERS

MILLS & BOON®

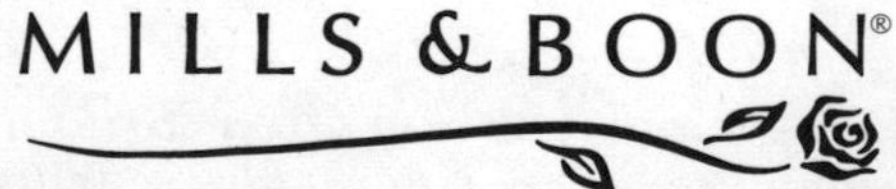

First published in Great Britain 1999
Large Print edition 2000
Harlequin Mills & Boon Limited,
Eton House, 18-24 Paradise Road,
Richmond, Surrey TW9 1SR

ISBN 0 263 16373 3

Set in Times Roman 16½ on 18 pt.
16-0002-49220

Printed and bound in Great Britain
by Antony Rowe Ltd, Chippenham, Wiltshire

CHAPTER ONE

FROM THE STEPS of the Trappist monastery on the hillside, Fran Mallory could see out over the entire Salt Lake Valley. At seven in the morning, the sun had barely come up over the mountains behind the sandy rock-faced edifice.

Dew still bathed the freshly mown grass on this glorious late April morning. A feeling of peace pervaded the grounds covered in acres of clover and flowering trees.

All this and more she'd been cataloguing with her camera as the delicious perfume of fruit blossoms acted like an aphrodisiac on her senses. She stood gazing at the clouds which moved across a brilliant blue sky like huge, fat white pillows piled as high as the eye could see.

Living by the dictates of a hectic agenda, she wished there were some way to store this moment as she would a piece of information on her computer, then come back to this exact spot with a click of the mouse whenever she needed to regroup and get in touch with her real self, whatever that was....

So far, she had no idea. Fran only knew that at rare times like this, her soul yearned inexplicably for something she couldn't put a name to.

As she stood there musing, the haunting sound of the monks singing Gregorian chant permeated the outside walls of the chapel. The beautiful male voices came from those celibate men who were dedicated to a higher cause in the service of God.

She couldn't fathom men who denied themselves their earthly passions in order to show their devotion.

On the other hand, her own selfish father hadn't been able to control his passions. After being unfaithful to her mother with more than one woman, he'd left the state never to be seen or heard from again.

Fran wasn't the only girl among her group of friends whose family had known tragedy. Marsha Hume's father was serving time in prison because it was discovered he'd been married to two women at the same time living in separate towns.

Fran hadn't been able to fathom that either. Nor could she countenance that several male students in her classes at the university turned out to be married men who'd come on to her while they'd been studying, actually believing she might be interested. Revolted and disillusioned, Fran found her distrust of men in general was growing.

If God had wanted man and woman to be married and cling happily together as one flesh forever, she didn't see it happening in the world she inhabited. Grudgingly she admitted there were a few exceptions. Her uncle and her pastor—and a couple of men at her work.

The monks she could hear singing could be added to the list. She supposed they were honorable men, although she put them in another classification of human being altogether.

She would sell her soul for one good man, but after twenty-eight years, she despaired of ever finding him. Tossing her head with its silvery-gold mane, she opened the heavy door, anxious to put aside any irritating thoughts on such a lovely day.

The chapel foyer appeared to be deserted. She shouldn't have been surprised. It was far too early in the day for visitors or tourists.

A sign indicated that guests should go upstairs to observe the mass. Another sign pointed to the gift shop on her right. Paul had said the Abbot would meet her in there for the initial interview. Depending on the outcome and his willingness, she might get some inside shots as well.

As Fran opened the gift shop door, her breath caught in her throat. After everything Paul had told her, she had been prepared to greet a man in his seventies.

The tall, dark-haired, clean-shaven monk behind the counter had to be in his midthirties. He was dressed in the same kind of brown work shirt and trousers she'd seen the monks wearing out in the orchards. Despite his attire, he had a princely bearing.

At her entry, he stopped stacking jars and flicked his dark, piercing gaze to hers. His intelligent eyes looked black but were probably brown. The dim light in the shop obscured details. After an unnerving silence she heard him murmur, "May I help you?"

This monk spoke in a deep, rich masculine tone, unaccountably stirring her senses.

"I'm Ms. Mallory from *Beehive Magazine*. The Abbot made arrangements to let someone from our magazine interview him for an article we want to run in the July issue. I was told to meet him here at seven."

"I'm afraid Father Ambrose is unwell this morning. He hopes you will forgive him for the inconvenience and make another appointment."

He went on filling the rest of the shelves with the kinds of jars of honey and jams she'd occasionally purchased here in past years.

"Of course."

Fran had never been this totally ignored before, but then again, she'd never come face-to-face with a Trappist monk either.

"Do I make it through you?"

He lifted his well-shaped head and stared at her, his eyes narrowing as if he were not pleased with the question.

"No. Phone him in a week. He should be better by then."

"I hope it's not serious."

"I shouldn't think so." He turned his back on her, no doubt signaling that this meeting had come to an end. Oddly enough she didn't want to go. The monks fascinated her, especially this one. His short-cropped hair looked boyish from the back. She tried to imagine him in jeans and T-shirt, his hair a normal length.

"I thought Trappist monks took vows of silence, the Abbot being the exception to handle the public, of course. Why is it that you can talk to me?"

"Though the brothers find excessive conversation unnecessary, the vow of total silence is a myth," came the even reply over his broad shoulder.

Fran didn't know that.

"If it's true, could I interview you while you work? Or is the Abbot the only one allowed to talk to women?"

"If that were the case, I wouldn't be speaking to you now," he answered quietly. Too quietly.

"I'm sorry. I didn't mean for that comment to sound provocative."

Suddenly he turned and faced her once more. "Why apologize?"

At the boldness of his question, she had no comeback because a river of heat unexpectedly coursed through her body.

"You're not the first curious woman to cross over this threshold, intrigued by a man's decision to remain celibate. No doubt someone with your looks would find that decision incomprehensible."

"*My* looks?" She could feel her indignation kindling.

"Come now, Ms. Mallory. You know very well your impact on a man, otherwise you would have framed your question differently." His gaze dropped lower. "You would have dressed in something less appealing. Only a woman with your kind of confidence lets nothing get in her way, not even the indisposition of Father Ambrose."

If she were a violent person, she would have slapped him. "I'm not surprised you've ended up in here, shut away from the world. Only God would be able to forgive your arrogance, not to mention your colossal rudeness to a stranger."

"You've left out a number of my major sins. In any event, I apologize for offending you."

"You don't talk like a monk."

His hands stilled on the counter. "How does a monk talk?"

She didn't have an answer for that. She had never known one. Paul had arranged things with the Abbot. In her opinion they were a different breed of men, wanting to be cloistered away from the world to worship.

"I'm sorry if I've shattered your illusions, but monks are ordinary people of flesh and blood. In some cases they're just as prone to flaws as the rest of the world."

"So I'm discovering." His frankness had come as a complete shock. "Is that what you want me to include in my article?" she challenged when she could find her voice.

"What I want is immaterial. Without Father Ambrose's consent, there won't be one."

"And if you could influence his decision, he wouldn't agree to make another appointment. It may interest you to know that I was sent on this assignment because a colleague from the magazine doing this part of the layout is ill with the flu. I didn't come here with the intention of giving sex-starved celibates their thrill for the morning.''

With her cheeks glowing hot she added, ''Judging by your reaction, it appears my presence has titillated you. No doubt your tortured conscience will force you to give yourself some sort of penance which you richly deserve.''

At the entry to the room she paused to shift her camera to her other shoulder. ''Tell the Abbot that someone from the magazine will call to make another appointment. Have a good day.''

She overcame the urge to slam the door in his face, then left the monastery without looking back. Her joy in the beauty of the morning had evaporated as if it had never been.

Andre Benet could smell the faint scent of peaches from her shampoo which lingered in the air after she stormed out of the gift shop.

He'd been rude to her. Exceedingly rude, yet he couldn't summon any guilt. She wasn't that different from his own birth mother, a woman who lit her own fires. A bewitching woman who went where angels feared to tread and never counted the cost.

His own mother had known of his father's proclivity for the priesthood, yet she'd tempted him before he'd gone away. Andre had been the result.

He wondered if it was a coincidence that Ms. Mallory had worn a peach-colored, two-piece suit. Even her skin had the proverbial peaches and cream glow. Combine this with gossamer hair, and no man would be totally immune, not even a monk, and she knew it!

Apparently his mother had possessed that same kind of haunting beauty and allure. Enough for his father to sleep with her one more time before he went his separate way.

Andre understood that kind of desire well enough. If he were an artist, he wouldn't be able to resist capturing the vision of Ms. Mallory on canvas. But he wasn't an artist, and certainly no monk.

As far as he knew, he had no particular talents. Orphaned at birth, he'd been raised in New Orleans by his Aunt Maudelle, an embittered but basically good woman who worked as a seamstress.

Enamored of the big boats traveling up and down the Mississippi, he had left home in his teens to see the world, working on freighters in various capacities until he'd become a merchant seaman.

In time he became good friends with a Swiss who spoke four languages fluently. Envious of his friend's ability, Andre enrolled at the university in Zurich where he studied German and French along with history. Though he could have gone into teaching with his degree, Andre returned to the sea, a job that allowed him latitude to keep on the move.

He stayed in touch with Maudelle and always sent her money. On the rare occasion, he came home to New Orleans for a short visit, but nothing could anchor his soul or curb his restlessness, certainly not a wife. Females were to be enjoyed, nothing more. Maudelle despaired of his attitude and prayed daily for his spiritual welfare.

He always laughed, but his amusement had vanished when a month ago a close friend of his aunt's actually spent the money to phone him aboard ship along the Bosporus and beg him to come home. His aunt was ill.

Andre had a gut feeling it might be fatal. Taking the next flight out of Ankara, Turkey, he found her on the point of death. Though he had never been a churchgoer and had no religious views, he knew she was a good Catholic so he called her parish for someone to come and administer the last rites.

While he held her hand and waited for a priest to appear, Maudelle began her confession. He had heard of deathbed repentance, but he'd never given it any thought. Not until certain revelations began pouring from her mouth.

Her confession had turned Andre's life inside out and had brought him to Salt Lake City, Utah, a place he had always thought of as the back of beyond, a wasteland the hated Mormon Pioneers of the 1840s had been driven to found during America's Western Expansion, a place no one else on earth wanted.

Andre loved the water.

The great Salt Lake Desert with its great Salt Sea was anathema to him. Yet here he was on temporary leave from his job…a stranger in a strange land…living in undreamed-of circumstances.

He could scarcely credit that he was really alive, except for the lingering scent of peaches which was a powerful reminder of his mortality. And, of course, the ailing monk lying down in his cell-like room at the other end of the sanctuary. A monk known to the world as Abbot Ambrose, Andre's biological father, born Charles Ambrose sixty-six years earlier to parents of English and French heritage.

According to Father Joseph, recurring bouts of pneumonia had aged his father a good ten years. The gaunt, frail monk was a shell of his former self.

As Andre let himself inside the room, his father turned his head and stared up at him. "Did you show the journalist around?"

"No. I told her you'd be better in a week. You've spent your life's work building this monastery to what it is today. No one else should give her your story but you."

His father lifted his hand. "I have done nothing. It is all God's handiwork, my son."

"Whatever you say, Father. Nevertheless, we'll let you get your strength back so you can be the one to guide the interview."

"I won't recover this time."

''Nonsense,'' Andre snapped. To lose the father he had just found, the parent he desperately wanted and needed to get to know, was killing him. ''I'm sending an ambulance for you. You should be in a hospital and waited on.''

''No.'' The older man wheezed, struggling for breath. ''No hospital for me. I always hated them.''

Another thing Andre and his father had in common.

So many things.

So many years gone by that they had been denied a knowledge of each other.

''You're my greatest earthly comfort now. Come closer. It's a joy to talk to the son of my flesh. You're a divine gift at my last hour.''

That had to be a lie.

Andre's sudden appearance at the monastery ten days ago announcing that he was the Abbot's son, had come as such a great shock, Andre was convinced his pneumonia had taken a turn for the worse.

No matter how much his father denied it, Andre knew the truth. He was the one responsible for the older man's present condition. It weighted Andre with fresh grief.

"You are not to blame for anything, my son. Indeed, you are a victim, and my heart grieves that you've been robbed of your family.

"If there is an accusing finger, it should be pointed at me for taking my pleasure with your mother before I said my final vows to become a monk. It was the most selfish thing I have ever done, and entirely unfair to you and your mother."

Andre's head reared back. "According to Aunt Maudelle, my mother tempted you beyond your endurance."

He raised his hand once more, then it fell back at his side. "Maudelle was your mother's elder sister. She never married, never knew a man. Her jealousy of Lisette made her say unkind things.

"Don't believe her accusations. A man cannot be tempted unless he allows himself to be, my son. You've been in the world. You know that's true."

Andre *did* know.

"Your mother's family was French. She was very beautiful. I see so much of Lisette in your black hair, your eyes,'' he cried softly before the coughing took over. ''Though I had always wanted to serve God, I loved her, too. My heart was torn because of conflicting loyalties.

''If she had let me know she was pregnant with you, I would have married her. Maybe a part of me was hoping it would happen. I told her I was being sent to Utah, but she remained silent. I never saw or heard from her again. I had no idea she died of complications after you were born.'' Tears rolled down his flushed cheeks.

''Make no mistake, Andre,'' he said in a hoarse voice. ''Your mother was the unselfish one. She deliberately chose not to tell me she was pregnant because in her heart, she knew of my desire to serve God. Otherwise why wouldn't I have married her rather than enroll in the seminary in the first place?

''In the end, your Aunt Maudelle did something even more unselfish. Despite her shortcomings and her jealousy, she raised you to be a wonderful man.''

''She didn't even have me christened with your name, Father.''

‘‘That wasn’t her fault. I’m sure she and your mother decided you should bear your mother’s name so there would be no scandal attached to my family name. Don’t you see? They wanted to protect me.

‘‘But Benet is a very fine name. Your mother’s name. Be proud of it. Oh, Andre— I don’t deserve such a blessing, but I do know God will reward Maudelle who must have secretly loved you like her own child. Just look at you!’’

He stared at Andre out of loving eyes. ‘‘I am so proud of you. You’ve been everywhere, done everything. You’re so knowledgeable about everything, you speak other languages. You’ve acquired a formal education, and have invested your money wisely. No man could ask for a finer son. I’ve told the brothers that you are my true-born son. I want to shout it to the world!’’

‘‘You shouldn’t have done that, Father. No one need have known. I never meant to bring you shame.’’

‘‘Shame?’’ He sounded truly angry. ‘‘You don’t understand! Why would I hide anything as miraculous as my own flesh and blood from the brothers I have served all these years? I've told them that when I'm gone, I want you to be free to stay here for as long as you like. This can be your home when you want it to be.

"I'm not a man of the world. I can't leave you a shop or a farm. I own nothing. But I can give you a quiet place of repose where you can come to be alone, to ponder. I see only one thing lacking in you. You've learned everything except the meaning of life. Maybe one day you'll find it here. Then you'll enjoy the peace which has eluded you for so long."

Andre marveled at his father's insight and grasped the frail hand reaching for his. When he heard his father sob, it was like a dam bursting. Andre broke down and wept with him.

"Andre?" he whispered some time later. "I know what's in your heart. Besides the confusion and anger you feel against me, your mother, your Aunt Maudelle, you have questions. I'll try my best to answer them all.

"But you must promise me something in return." Another battle for breath wracked his body.

"Andre—promise me you'll not let anger and bitterness rule your life!"

His father was asking the impossible, but with Death holding her jaws open wide, Andre didn't see he had a choice and gave his newly found parent the one promise he couldn't imagine keeping.

Fran couldn't believe it was the middle of May already. Friday was the deadline for the July issue, and she still had to make that trip out to Clarion today to visit some of the descendants of the first Jewish settlers to the state and get pictures.

"Line two for you, Frannie."

"I can't take it right now, Paula."

"But the man called five times yesterday."

"What's his name?"

"He wouldn't leave it. I told him you would be in for a few minutes this morning and now I've run out of excuses."

"Oh, all right."

She hated it when people refused to be called back, as if she lived to answer their phone calls. Pushing the hair away from her face, she put the receiver to her ear. ''Fran Mallory here.''

''Ms. Mallory. At last.''

Fran recognized that voice.

Without volition her body started to tremble for a variety of reasons she couldn't explain. One thing was certain. Trappist monk or no, she refused to help him out. If that was uncharitable, then so be it. He'd been horrible to her.

''Yes?'' came her sharp reply.

''I deserved that.''

The unexpected olive branch caused her eyes to close tightly. Never in her life had she met a person less like a monk, even if she hadn't personally known one.

''If the Abbot is well enough to handle an interview, you should be talking to Paul Goates. It's his story.''

''I understand he's on vacation. If you still want to do the article, come to the monastery now.''

The line went dead.

She held the receiver in front of her and let out a cry of frustration before banging it down on the hook.

"Come to the monastery now," she mimicked him in a Darth Vader voice. Who did he think he was? The divine vessel?

"Talking to yourself again, Frannie? You know what that's a sign of," Paul baited her.

Paul!

She swung around in her swivel chair. "What are you doing here?"

The short blond journalist blinked. "Last I knew, I happened to work here."

"But you're on vacation."

"I am? Did Barney finally give me a break? Now? When we're this close to the deadline? That's news to me."

"That monk from the monastery just called and said I should come for the interview right now. He said you were out of town."

"I was. Yesterday." Paul broke out in a grin. "That monk must want to see you again. If you can't imagine how hard up they are for the sight of a good-looking woman, I can."

Paul was wrong. The particular monk in question didn't like women. She had firsthand knowledge of that salient fact.

"Well, I'm certainly not going back there again when it's your story, Paul."

"Ah, come on. Give the poor guy a break." He winked. "Besides, I'm due at the Dinosaur Museum out in Vernal by noon to get pictures on that new set of Brontosaurus fossils for the July edition. And don't forget, you've already taken outside photos of the monastery.

"They were fabulous, by the way. In fact some of those wide-angled lens shots capturing the mountains were inspired. It's all yours with my blessing, Frannie baby."

"Thanks a lot," she muttered, not in the least happy about the sudden change in plans. She almost dreaded seeing him again, though in her heart of hearts she had to admit the monk fascinated her. He made her feel things she'd never felt before and couldn't put a name to. The only saving grace was the fact that she'd be in the Abbot's company for the duration of the interview.

As for the monk, she could pray he wouldn't be anywhere around. If she did happen to bump into him, she would pretend he wasn't alive.

But a half hour later she had to recant those words when she discovered him waiting for her in the parking lot of the monastery grounds. Before the car had even come to a stop, the adrenaline was surging through her veins.

He opened the door on the driver's side and took the camera case from her. Heat suffused her face as she felt his glance on her long, shapely legs where her dress had ridden up. She quickly got out of the car, noticing that he was dressed in the same dark work pants and matching shirt he'd worn the other day.

On her first visit, she hadn't realized how tan he was. The gift shop had been too dim. In the strong sunlight, his skin looked burnished to teak, witness of the many hours he spent in the out-of-doors. His dark aquiline features and strong, hard-muscled body took her breath. Embarrassed to be caught staring, she averted her eyes.

"You must have surpassed the speed limit to have arrived here this fast, Ms. Mallory."

"I'm on a deadline. This stop is only one of several I have to make today, but I suppose that to you it's another sin you can lay at my feet."

"Another?"

"No doubt you've compiled a long list by now."

"Why would I do that?" He shut the door for her.

"Why, indeed. Is the Abbot waiting inside?"

"No. He passed away four days after your visit."

Fran let out a shocked gasp. "I don't understand. Why didn't you tell me this when you phoned?"

"Why?" He stroked his strong chin. "Surely his death could mean nothing to you. You'll still get your story."

She turned on the monk, her hands curled into fists. "How can you say that? Paul told me that over the phone he came across as a wonderful, delightful person. I was looking forward to meeting him and am very saddened by the news."

"I stand rebuked," he murmured.

She swallowed hard. As an apology, it wasn't much. But obviously this monk had never developed any social graces.

"I understand he was the Abbot here for over thirty years. Being that you monks live in such a close community, I can only assume that he'll be terribly missed."

"I'm sure he will."

"You're mocking me."

He gave a careless, yet elegant shrug of his shoulders. "Not at all. On the contrary, I shall miss him more than you know," he said in a raw voice that oddly enough lent credence to his words. Maybe the Abbot's illness and death had brought out the worst in him.

Hadn't she read somewhere that nuns and monks weren't supposed to become attached to each other? In Fran's mind, a person would have to be pretty inhuman not to care.

"Father Ambrose honored me by asking if I would handle this interview in his place."

Something was going on here. Some strange undercurrent she didn't understand, but she had no desire to fence further with this enigmatic monk.

"Our magazine would love to honor him and his memory."

"Tell me about the magazine you work for, Ms. Mallory."

"We print a monthly publication that sells Utah to the world. We do in-depth articles on geographical locations of interest, history, religion, industry, recreational sites, people.''

``Why a story on the monastery after all these years?''

``We want to devote an issue to Utah, then and now. It will include stories about the diverse groups of people still here today who can trace their roots back to pioneer times.

``As I understand it, this monastery got its start in the 1860s, but the first wooden structure burned to the ground from a lightning strike. I researched enough to find out that it didn't become a truly self-sufficient community until a hundred years later when Abbot Ambrose was sent here. Now it's a place of beauty and a sanctuary for those who visit as well as those who make up its religious community.''

``I'm impressed you know that much about it. I suggest we start the interview by taking a walk through the orchards.''

For the first time since they'd met, he seemed a little less defensive. This in turn helped her to relax somewhat. ``If it's all right with you, I'll turn on my tape recorder as we talk.''

He nodded. She had to walk fast to keep up with his long strides. He moved with an effortless male grace she couldn't help admiring. "Were the orchards his idea?"

"Yes, those and the beehives, both of which brought in enough revenue from their homemade honey butter and preserves to purchase more land and sustain the community without any funds from the outside."

"Where did he get his recipes?"

"The Abbot grew up in Louisiana. He had a friend whose mother cooked for a wealthy white family who owned one of the plantations and used it to entertain friends on the weekend. Apparently the boys would watch her make jam and honey butter. He brought the secret of good old Southern cooking with him."

"The honey butter is fabulous. I often buy it. What a fantastic story. Oh, I would have loved to have talked to the Abbot in person."

"He was far too ill at the end to grant anyone an interview. But I can tell you this much. When he arrived here thirty years ago, there was nothing but a Quonset hut left over from World War II set on a plot of ground filled with rocks and weeds."

She stopped in her tracks and looked out over the lush vista before her, snapping photo after photo of the brothers at work. Slowly her eyes traveled to the monastery itself. ''The rocks in the facade—''

''All of it local stone. Each one was manually hoisted and carried by the monks to build the new structure. It was a painstaking, tedious process. A labor of love that took many years.''

''The Abbot had vision to make this all work,'' she surmised aloud. ''What a remarkable monk. Are there any photos showing the way it looked when he first started building the new chapel?''

''There are a few, but they're not in very good condition.''

''We have an expert on the staff who does excellent restoration work. Would you trust me with them? If not, I can consult someone at the Utah Historical Society and see what they have on hand.''

''I see no reason why you can't borrow them.''

Secretly Fran was delighted. For some odd reason she wanted this article to be exceptional.

"Is it permitted to take any pictures inside the church?"

"You can take photos in several places. From the loft where the public is allowed to witness the mass, you should be able to get your best shots of the altar. He had the small Pieta specially commissioned from Florence, Italy."

"I've seen it before. It's exquisite. Do you think I could take pictures of it as well as the Abbot's grave? I presume he's buried on the property. I'd like a picture of his headstone to finish the article and entitle it, 'Monument to a saint.'"

The monk's expression sobered. In a quiet voice he said, "The community cemetery is behind the monastery."

For the next hour Fran plied him with questions as they toured the grounds, the kitchen, the library which the Abbot used for his personal study, and the inner sanctuary. Naturally the monks' dormitory was off limits.

When they reached the gift store, she took more pictures, then bought honey butter and pear jam to give to her family. She also took some free literature which contained facts she would intersperse in the article.

"I have one more favor to ask." He had walked her out to the car. The time had flown and she found herself reluctant to leave. "You've let me photograph your brothers. May I take one last picture of you on the chapel steps?"

"No."

It was unequivocal and final.

A wave of disappointment swept through her but she determined not to show it. *What's wrong with you, Fran? He's a monk, for heaven's sake!*

Forcing a smile she looked up at him. "You've been more generous with your time and information than I would have expected. I'll leave so you can get back to your duties. I-I never realized how hard you work, how busy you are."

She knew she was talking too fast, but she couldn't help it. Whenever she got nervous, the words sort of tumbled out.

"This has been an education for me. I know it will make fascinating reading for thousands of people. When the proofs are ready, I'll call you and show you a mockup of the layout for your approval."

"When will that be?"

She had to think fast. There was still the drive to Clarion to fit in. If she worked late—

"Day after tomorrow." Deadline day. "Probably nine o'clock. Will that be convenient for you?"

"I'll be in the gift store."

I know.

That's the problem. I'm afraid I'm not going to forget.

What excuse will I have for showing up here after the article has been published and you've been furnished a copy?

"All this time and you've never told me the name you go by."

His features closed up. "It's not important."

He held the driver's door open so she was forced to get in. When he shut it, he said, "I've been following Father Ambrose's instructions.

Just pretend he was the one giving you the interview. God will forgive this one lie.''

Her hands gripped the steering wheel tightly. His words implied that God wouldn't forgive anything else.

Was it a warning?

Had he sensed her natural attraction to him? Had he felt it from the first moment they'd met?

If he worked in the gift shop, how many female visitors to the monastery had been drawn to his dark looks and undeniable masculine appeal? Is that why he'd been so rude to her?

Mortified that this might be the case, she refused to look at him and drove away, her face on fire. But as she rounded the curve at the bottom of the drive, she couldn't help looking in the rearview mirror one last time. He wasn't there.

CHAPTER TWO

"AUNT MAUDELLE? What was my daddy like?"

"How do I know. Your mother went with a lot of different men. All I can say is, he wasn't around when you were born."

"I made her die, huh."

"Not on purpose. Now stop asking questions and finish the dishes. It's time for bed and I'm tired. We've got to go to mass in the morning."

"What's mass?"

"Church."

"I don't like church. It's spooky."

"You're not supposed to like it."

"Why not?"

"Duty is different than pleasure. It builds character."

"What's character?"

"It's doing something you don't want to do."

"Then why do we have to do it?"

"Why? Because God said so."

"What's God?"

"Don't you know?"

"I know who Mary is."

"Who is she?"

"She's Jesus's mommy. He was lucky 'cause he got to see her all the time."

"Who told you that?"

"Pierre. I wish I could see my mommy."

"Well you can't, so stop fussing about it."

"Okay."

Andre came awake from his bad dreams with a jerk. His skin glistened with perspiration. He checked his watch. It was four-thirty in the morning.

He levered himself from the cot in the sparsely furnished room used by guests of the monastery. Pouring water into a bowl, he sluiced his face with the cold liquid, then raked his hands through his hair to steady them.

For the first time in his life it occurred to him that he had never dreamed about missing his father, only his mother. How strange. Even stranger and crueler was Aunt Maudelle's silence. All those years growing up and she never said a word.

But after his long talks with his father, he began to understand how much it must have hurt his aunt that he didn't show more appreciation for her sacrifice. Every time he told her he missed his mother, she must have suffered because she had tried so hard to be a mother to him.

Part of him wished he had never heard her confession. Now it was too late to go back and tell his aunt how sorry he was that he hadn't understood.

Wasn't there an old adage about ignorance being bliss?

Up until her confession, his life hadn't necessarily been blissful, but he had made a comfortable living, most of which had been invested. There was no question that he'd been able to pursue his education and continue the adventurous lifestyle he craved.

Now suddenly he was grounded for the moment to a piece of land no man owned, in a landlocked desert which might as well be on another planet.

If he had felt no sense of identity before Aunt Maudelle's confession, he felt it even less now that he'd come face to face with his own father.

They were total opposites.

His father loved the Rocky Mountains. He loved growing things. A flower, a four-leaf clover, those were miracles to him. He craved the stability of one location. A simple man with simple tastes who liked to work with his hands and accepted his daily lot without question. A cheerful, obedient, temperate individual who didn't need a woman. A man who believed God existed.

How could Andre have come from such a man?

For that matter, how could he have come from a mother who had no schooling past the eighth grade, who had no dreams, who was forced to go to mass once a week and was content to sew dresses for wealthy ladies?

According to his father she was a beautiful young woman who had many admirers, but fell in love with a man who wanted to be a monk. None of it made sense to Andre.

Possibly this was how some adopted children felt when they learned about the lives of their birth parents. They simply couldn't relate.

He wiped his jaw with a towel, noting the rasp of his beard. A shave was in order. He'd get cleaned up when it was time to meet with Ms. Mallory at nine. Once he had approved the layout of her article, he would send for a taxi and head for the airport.

No matter how kind the brothers had been, he was a stranger here. It was time to move on.

However, as long as he had come to the States, he decided now would be the right time to fly to Los Angeles and sign on a freighter making runs to Alaska, a place he had never visited. New sights were what he needed. For the time being, he craved the open sea, particularly the calm, sunny waters of the Pacific.

At a loose end, he decided to dress and join the brothers out in the orchard. They were up and on the job by five. Three or four hours of hard labor would make the time go faster. In the mood he was in, a book wouldn't hold him. It was better to keep physically busy so he wouldn't think.

Throughout Andre's extensive travels he'd met many exotic, mysterious women. He'd had relationships with several of them. But living at the monastery with his ailing father had been a different proposition altogether.

Apart from being at sea for long periods with the men, he supposed this was the longest time he had ever gone without having the slightest interest in a woman. Therefore he had to assume that Ms. Mallory's image kept intruding because unlike the other female visitors to the monastery, he linked her presence with his father and knew she would be back to finish up the interview.

Four hours later the woman in question walked into the gift shop with a large folder tucked beneath her arm. Andre was not pleased to discover that he'd been listening for her footsteps. Nor was he very happy about the sudden race of his pulse when he finally acknowledged her presence.

So much for following in his celibate father's footsteps.

She wasn't the most beautiful woman he'd ever seen in his life. But there was something different about her. Even in the dim light, she glowed with health, as if she'd brought the essence of the day with her. That had to be the missing ingredient in the others.

"Good morning." Her voice had taken on a husky tone that reached to his insides.

"Ms. Mallory. Go ahead and lay it on the counter." He moved a few jars to make room.

She opened the folder, then turned it to face him. "As you can see, there's a colored picture of Father Ambrose at the head of the article. The archives department of the Catholic administrative offices donated it.

"I understand it was taken at least twenty years ago. He was a very handsome man in his robes. You've been so kind to allow us to do the article, I had the original framed as a gift for the monastery. It's m—the magazine's way of thanking you for your time."

Andre caught the brief slip she'd made before she propped the framed picture on the counter next to the folder. His thoughts reeled as he stared into the burnished face and dark blue eyes of the man who had sired him.

One look erased the haunting memory of the much older, worn-out monk who had struggled with every breath until he'd died in Andre's arms.

Ms. Mallory had spoken the truth.

In his father's younger days, he'd been a good-looking man. He stood tall in his monkly vestments, and appeared very distinguished. An unexpected rush of filial pride shook Andre to the core.

Those leaf-green eyes of hers darted him an anxious glance. "I-Is it all right?"

He cleared his throat. "Yes," came the gruff response. Andre no longer felt the desire to bait her, particularly not when she'd given him a gift beyond price.

There was a slight hesitation before she murmured, "Please— take your time looking over the article and pictures. I'm going for a walk. I'll be back shortly."

He didn't know if she was just being sensitive to his mood, or if she needed to use the ladies' room, but he was grateful for a few minutes alone.

Once she'd left, he read every word, marveling over her grasp of his father's life's work. The photos captured the tranquillity and beauty of the church and its surroundings.

A deep pain seared him because his modest parent hadn't been able to hang on long enough to enjoy reading this wonderful tribute to the monastic life and his contribution to the community in general.

The article made his father come alive in a brand-new way. Deep in thought, he hadn't realized that Ms. Mallory had come back in the room until he caught the flowery scent of her perfume.

"Is there anything you want changed? Anything you don't agree with?" Her eyes searched his.

"No. If the Abbot were alive, he would have cherished this."

"I'm glad," she said quietly before looking away. "When it's published, I'll bring several copies for everyone."

I won't be here, Andre mused to himself. "The brothers will be pleased."

He heard her suck in her breath. "Good. Then I won't keep you any longer. I need to get back to the office straightaway. Goodbye."

She closed the file folder and put it under her arm. The action drew his attention to the alluring shape of her body beneath the yellow suit before she started out of the room.

Andre should have answered her, but the word stuck in his gullet. Rather than escort her outside, he remained behind the counter, as if it were his refuge.

One less memory to deal with.

Andre didn't like Salt Lake and had no intention of coming back.

Fran might have had a dozen errands to run in preparation for her upcoming assignment to cover the Salt Lake Mormon Tabernacle Choir's tour to Los Angeles and Australia. But she'd been counting the minutes until the July issue of *Beehive Magazine* was off the press. She hadn't slept all night waiting for this morning so she could take several copies to the monastery.

After her last trip out there, she'd made up her mind that she would send the magazines in the mail. It would be the right thing to do. The moral thing to do considering she'd been having fantasies about a Trappist Monk.

But some force beyond her will couldn't or wouldn't let it go at that.

I have to see the monk one more time. I have to.

Her mother would be shocked if she knew the truth. Fran herself was shocked by her own behavior.

If the pastor of her church knew, he would tell Fran the adversary was devious and knew how to get to people when they were at their most vulnerable. She'd heard it all before from the pulpit, but had never placed any credence in those words.

She still didn't. But there was no doubt in her mind that going to see the monk *this* time was wrong.

"You're not the first curious female to cross over this threshold, intrigued by a man's decision to remain celibate. No doubt someone with your looks would find that decision incomprehensible."

Fran's face always went hot when she was embarrassed or ashamed. It was hot now just remembering those words.

The monk had known more about her than she had known about herself. Indeed he had very calculatingly revealed her to herself without batting an eye.

What was really humiliating was the fact that she was going back to the scene of the crime, possibly for more of the same treatment. Was she a masochist, or simply a twisted woman who craved this celibate monk's attention though she would deny it to her dying breath?

Even though there were eighty or so monks in residence, she only brought a couple of dozen copies. The brothers weren't allowed to keep any personal possessions, so an individual copy wasn't necessary. But this way there would be enough to circulate and still keep several on hand in the gift shop for any visitor interested in learning more about the history of the religious shrine.

Now that it was the first of July, different trees were in flower on the monastery grounds. The brothers had to be worn out working in this intense ninety-degree heat. During her interview, she had discovered that there was no air-conditioning inside. Fran couldn't imagine living without refrigeration.

She couldn't imagine living at a monastery, period!

This time when she parked her car, she noticed other cars and a Greyhound touring bus.

People were milling about. This meant there would be more tourists inside the gift shop.

A frown drove her delicately arched eyebrows together. She hadn't counted on an audience when she delivered her gift.

You wanted to be alone with him.

Francesca Mallory, you're a fool!

Without another moment's hesitation she got out of the car and started for the chapel entrance, the magazines in her arm.

As she had suspected, the gift shop teemed with people in sunglasses, carrying cameras, buying everything in sight. Two elderly monks waited on people, but the one who haunted her nights was nowhere in sight.

Her heart dropped to her toes. She waited in the corner until most of the room had emptied before approaching the one closest to her.

"I'm Fran Mallory from *Beehive Magazine.* I told the monk who granted me the interview on Abbot Ambrose that I would bring by some copies for all of you."

He gave a slight bow. "You're very kind." Then he reached for the magazines. This wasn't going the way she had planned it. Now she had little choice but to hand them over.

''Would it be possible to speak to the monk I interviewed?''

''He's no longer with us.''

Fran blinked in astonishment. ''You mean he's been sent to another monastery?'' she cried before she could stop herself.

''I'm not at liberty to say.''

Her skin prickled unpleasantly. ''Of course not. I only meant that I'm disappointed that I couldn't thank him in person for all his help.''

''I'll pass the message along.''

''Th-Thank you. Goodbye.''

''Goodbye.''

Shaken by the news, Fran hurried out to the car but didn't immediately start the motor.

The sense of loss was too staggering.

By the time she left for Los Angeles two days later, she was furious with herself for having allowed his memory to interfere with her work. As she boarded one of the two specially chartered 747s to carry the Choir and staff, she made up her mind to leave all thoughts of him behind and concentrate on her work.

This trip was not only going to be a great adventure, it was vitally important to her career. She wasn't about to jeopardize her work because of a monk she had no business thinking about.

With her mind made up, she found the excitement contagious as she, along with the Choir, arrived at Hollywood Bowl in Los Angeles by bus for their concert given to a sellout crowd.

Being a fan of the hundred-and-fifty-year-old Choir, Fran had attended dozens of their home concerts. For years she had listened to their international Sunday broadcasts, and was familiar with much of their repertoire. Certain songs thrilled her, others moved her to tears.

But there was one song in particular that always left her and the audience weeping. Afterwards, there would be this electric silence before the crowd rose to its feet in thunderous applause. To Fran, that awe-filled silence proved the greatest ovation of all.

Tonight she was ready with her camera to capture the enchanted expression of some attendee's face. The right picture always told the tale.

She wanted to find that one photograph which exuded the magic of the night. Barney was counting on her. If she were successful, it would go on the front cover of *Beehive Magazine,* a coup she hadn't yet accomplished, but maybe this time.

The song she'd been waiting for came soon after the intermission. She'd obtained permission to set things up near the orchestra where she would be out of the way, yet obtain frontal shots with her telephoto lens.

The choir leader stepped to the podium and raised his baton. When everything grew quiet, the sopranos began singing their moving entreaty. The heartrending music pierced a part of Fran's soul not reached in any other way. It happened every time, not just to her, but to everyone in the listening crowd.

Slowly she panned the audience, snapping one picture after another. By the time the full swell of male voices began, she happened on a face glowing with pure joy. There wasn't another word to describe it.

A woman in her midsixties maybe, gray hair, a sweet expression on what looked like her Eastern European features.

The tears rolled down her rosy cheeks. Her eyes seemed transfixed by the music.

Fran swallowed hard and took a dozen pictures in succession. There was no need to look anywhere else. Something told her that this woman was the one she'd been hoping to find in the audience, the one who reflected the feelings of everyone around.

Maybe Fran could find a subject this perfect in Australia, but she doubted it. The moment was an illuminating one. She felt the hairs stand on the back of her neck.

Driven by a compulsion she didn't understand, she was anxious for the concert to be over so she could approach the woman. There had to be a story behind that face. Fran wanted to get it, not only for the article, but out of a burning curiosity.

After the Choir sang their last number, the audience must have clapped for a solid five minutes. No one wanted the concert to be over.

With purposeful steps, Fran insinuated herself into the crowd and waited at the end of the row for the woman to exit. While everyone around was expounding on the remarkable performance they had just heard, Fran approached her.

''It was a beautiful concert, wasn't it?''

The woman whose face glistened with fresh tears threw her head back. ‘‘It was as wonderful as I remembered it back in Germany.’’

‘‘You heard the Choir there?’’

‘‘Oh, yes. Many years ago. When I was a little girl growing up in East Berlin, my mother told me that if I ever got the chance, I should get away to a place where I could be free to worship God. I didn’t know what she meant.

‘‘Then many years later came détente. I fled with my family to Frankfurt. It was there I heard this beautiful music for the first time. Later, when we moved to Zurich, in Switzerland, I heard the Choir again. That’s when I found God.’’ She shook her head. ‘‘You can’t imagine.’’

But Fran could. She’d even captured the woman’s ecstasy on film. ‘‘Thank you for sharing that with me,’’ she whispered. ‘‘I work for a magazine in Utah and have been taking pictures tonight. I took some of you. Do I have your permission to use them and your story?’’

The woman smiled. ‘‘I don’t mind.’’

‘‘Thank you,’’ Fran murmured as she watched the woman rejoin her family slowly making its way out of the row into the crowded aisle.

With her own eyes tear-drenched, Fran turned to go the other way and found herself face-to-face with a man who could have been the monk's twin, except that his hair was longer and he wore a suit and tie.

Hadn't she read somewhere that everyone on earth had a double?

There seemed to be an air of unreality about the entire evening. Her heart was really being given a workout. First the woman, now this haunting face from the past, a face she'd tried in vain to forget.

Angry with herself for staring at him, she averted her eyes and attempted to step past him.

''Ms. Mallory?''

Fran froze in place. That voice.

''If you're afraid I'm an apparition, I assure you I'm not.''

She whirled around, confused and disbelieving. ''When I took the magazines to the monastery, one of the monks told me you were no longer there. I had no idea you'd come to Los Angeles.''

"I left the day after your last visit."

Her breathing had grown too shallow. "I can't say I'm surprised. You didn't seem to fit the mold."

His lips twitched. "You're right about that."

Once again his honesty disarmed her. "Did you run away?"

There was an almost imperceptible nod of his dark head. "In a manner of speaking."

"Can a monk do that?" she cried softly. "I mean, aren't there certain formalities you have to go through if you want to leave your Order?"

"Endless formalities, including petitioning for a dispensation from the Pope in Rome."

Fran had only seen movies about nuns and monks. She had no idea about the process, except through film. She doubted Hollywood could ever produce a performance that portrayed the true anguish involved in such a decision, if one had been devout.

"H-Have you already been excommunicated?"

"Not to my knowledge."

By now most of the people were making their way out to their cars. It was a good thing. Her shock would have been visible to anyone watching or listening.

"Are you in torment over your decision?"

He cocked his head. "Are you worried about my immortal soul?"

She could stand anything but his mockery. "In a manner of speaking, yes!" She parroted his earlier comment. "After the unorthodox way you treated me when I first came to the monastery, I didn't see how you would survive there."

"So you did think about me."

Her eyes flashed. "You're twisting my words."

"I'm touched that you cared."

Fran couldn't take any more. Obviously the man had to be in pain, but it was nothing to do with her. "I'm sorry," she murmured. "I've been too outspoken. It's one of my worst faults."

"I find that fault refreshing."

She swallowed hard. "I had no right to say that to you. I don't know anything about you or your life. I'm just surprised to see you here of all places."

"Did you think I couldn't appreciate a concert such as this?"

"Of course not. The Gregorian chant I listened to at the monastery was some of the most beautiful music I've ever heard. But that isn't what I meant. "

"What did you mean then?"

"Surely I don't have to explain it to you. We both happen to be in Los Angeles at the same time. The odds of our running into each other like this must be in the millions."

"I was thinking the same thing when I discovered you talking to Gerda."

Fran gave a little gasp. "You know her?"

"We met a long time ago. When she found out I was going to be in Los Angeles, she and her family invited me to come hear the choir's performance with them."

He studied her upturned features with avid intensity. Fran's trembling legs would hardly hold her up.

"How is it you happened to talk to her out of all the people in the audience?" he asked.

"I'm here on assignment from the magazine to cover the choir's trip to Australia. Besides the write-up, I'll be taking pictures of faces in the audience, watching for reactions that will capture the essence of the Choir's performance.

"Tonight I found what I was looking for in your friend's expression. Thankfully, she gave me permission to use the pictures."

He appeared to ponder her words. She couldn't help but wonder what he was thinking that made him regard her with such solemnity. "You were fortunate then. She's a very special person."

Fran wondered where he had met the older woman, under what circumstances. Her curiosity about everything to do with him and his life was eating her alive.

"I felt that too."

"You'll be flying to Sydney tomorrow?"

"Yes. It will be the Choir's first stop in Australia."

"You'll like it."

"You've been there?" she blurted.

"I have."

When there was nothing else forthcoming she said, ‘‘Do you live in Los Angeles now?’’

His eyes were shuttered. ‘‘No.’’

She shouldn’t have asked him. As long as he was a monk, he was probably under some kind of constraint not to discuss anything personal, even if he wasn’t inside monastery walls.

That sense of loss was back, stronger than before.

‘‘I’m looking forward to visiting Brisbane.’’ She started talking faster and faster to cover her growing emptiness. ‘‘I h-hear the beaches are pristine, and the rain forest is magical.’’

‘‘All of it’s true. But whatever you do, be sure to take time out to visit the Great Barrier Reef. It’s spectacular.’’

‘‘So I’ve been told.’’ She cleared her throat. ‘‘For someone who has lived the monastic life, the world must be a place of continual fascination for you.’’

‘‘Oh, it is. And never more fascinating than right now.’’

With any other man she might have taken the comment personally. But this man was a monk who was still running away from something he couldn't reconcile. Among the many sensations he aroused, her compassion seemed to be at the forefront.

"I pray you'll eventually find what you're looking for."

One dark eyebrow quirked. "Are you a praying person?"

She took a deep breath. "It was a figure of speech."

"So you're not a praying person."

"I didn't say that."

"Then what were you trying to say?"

She'd had enough of this inquisition. "I'm not the one in the spiritual dilemma here. I need to go. The bus will be waiting. There aren't that many hours before we all have to be at the airport again."

"Goodbye again," he murmured. "Enjoy your trip."

She said goodbye in a quiet voice before turning on her heel to leave. It killed her that he could allow her to escape without calling her back. She had the awful premonition they would never see each other again.

What else did you expect? Did you honestly think a troubled monk would ask you to spend the rest of the night with him?

Why are you surprised, Francesca Mallory?

Why are you hurt? What could he possibly mean to you, or you to him?

Don't you know you're a stupid, stupid fool?

How many times must you have it drummed in your head before you get it?

CHAPTER THREE

"NOW THERE'S A SIGHT for sore eyes."

One of the shipmen, Jimmy Bing, lived in Los Angeles. His family was down there among the throngs waiting for him. Obviously home was where the heart was.

Andre had his own opinion. He'd sailed into many ports in his lifetime, but out of all of them, San Pedro left the most to be desired. Probably because the early September smog blanketing L.A. hung like a shroud over the sprawling metropolis.

"Where's your home, Andre?"

"I was born in New Orleans."

"You don't have a southern drawl."

"I left at an early age."

"With a name like yours, I figured you were from Quebec."

"A name like mine?"

"Yes. Benet. Before I got married and moved to L.A., I used to work the St.

Lawrence Seaway. One of the shipmen was a French-Canadian who had your last name."

"So you pegged me for a Canadian?"

"I don't know. You never hang out with them. You're kind of a loner. Like me." He grinned. "Are you going home for a while?"

Home? Where was that?

The question never used to bother him. But since Andre had watched his father's body being lowered into the ground by the brothers he'd served, the need to know more about who he was had been eating him alive.

"I'm doing another run to Alaska."

"When is the ship due to go back?"

"In a couple of days."

Jimmy hoisted his duffel bag over his shoulder. "Well, if I can't talk you into coming to my house, then I guess I'd better get a move on. My wife and kids are waiting for me." His eyes were alive with anticipation. "It's been a pleasure working with you, Andre."

Andre nodded. "I enjoyed your company too. Good luck, Jimmy."

A huge crowd had turned out to meet their ship. But Andre kept his eyes on Jimmy who descended the gangplank as fast as was humanly possible.

In the distance, he saw a pretty, red-headed mother holding the hands of her two children. They were all running toward him. Andre could hear their joyous shouts.

Soon he saw Jimmy lower his bag and throw his arms around the three of them. They clung.

Andre could feel their happiness. He had never envied anyone as much as he envied Jimmy at that moment. The picture became a blur. Suddenly Andre could hear his father talking.

"I'm not a man of the world, my son. I can't leave you a shop or a farm. I own nothing. But I can give you a quiet place of repose where you can come to be alone, to ponder. You haven't found the meaning of your life in your travels. Maybe one day you'll find it here. Then you'll enjoy the peace you've been searching for."

Andre grimaced, then grabbed his duffel bag and hurried ashore.

One thing was certain. Bumping into Ms. Mallory at Hollywood Bowl two months ago hadn't helped his state of mind. On top of everything else bothering him, she made him feel guilty for his sin of omission.

On those previous occasions in her presence, he'd had his reasons for not telling her the truth. They'd made perfect sense to him. But no longer.

Maybe the peace and quiet of the monastery was exactly what he needed to get his head on straight. It was only an hour's flight to Salt Lake. The brothers would give him the space he wanted.

Right now he craved privacy. Living at sea in such close quarters with the other men made that impossible.

Loners were perceived as troublemakers by virtue of their desire for isolation. A loner caused division in the group without meaning to. Division created unrest and low morale among the crew.

Andre was beginning to think that if he didn't snap out of it pretty soon, his days of working at sea were numbered.

Seven hours later, when the burning orange ball of the sun had long since dropped into the Great Salt Lake, he drove his rental car past the gates leading to the monastery.

The brothers had finished their chores for the day. Not a soul was in sight. Halfway to the edifice he pulled to the side of the road to finish his hamburger and fries.

When he looked up, the mountains seemed to jump out at him. The snow had melted from their peaks, evidence of a hot summer. He hadn't appreciated them on his first visit. They literally rose from the backyards of peoples' homes.

His father would have seen this view every day. For a man who had been born in the flat lands of the Louisiana Bayou, the rugged terrain of the Rockies must have been a constant source of amazement to him.

The peal of bells resounded from the church belfry, permeating the tranquillity of the well-tended grounds and orchards. It was a beautiful sound, if not a little lonely. But that was because Andre was on the outside, looking in. This was home to eighty monks who wanted for nothing. Each was content.

Andre was the visitor who didn't belong, but because of an accident of birth, he had the right to come and go here at will.

However, he didn't have the right to disturb the brothers any more than he could help. They retired early.

Starting up the motor once more, he continued his drive to the monastery and locked the car. The warm night air smelled sweet. It brought a physical ache clear to his hands.

With a tug of the bellpull, he summoned one of the brothers who greeted him cordially and told him he could use the same room as before.

A feeling of déjà vu accompanied him on his solitary walk through the corridors lined with holy pictures.

The sense of loss grew stronger. He'd had so little time with his parent.

His room appeared to be the same as he'd left it. With one exception. Someone had left a magazine on the desk next to the missal.

Curious, he put down his duffel bag and reached for it. ''*BEEHIVE MAGAZINE.* Your Passport to Utah's Wonders.''

He opened the cover and scanned the index. Francesca Mallory. His heart gave a hard kick.

Sinking down on the cot, he turned to the article on the monastery. The mockup she'd shown him hadn't done it justice.

Staring straight at him, taking up the whole page, was the full color picture of his father, Abbot Ambrose, the same picture he carried in his bag.

A lump lodged in his throat and refused to go away.

He read every word of the text several times.

When he thought about it, hundreds of millions of people had lived and died over the centuries, and no one ever knew their stories. Yet many thousands of people had already read this article which witnessed to the world that Andre's father had performed a special work on the earth and had made a remarkable contribution.

A feeling of gratitude for the owner of the magazine, for the woman who had penned the article in spite of his initial rudeness to her, swelled in his breast, taking away some of the sadness.

His spirits unaccountably lighter, he took a shower, then went to bed. Knowing he wouldn't fall asleep for a long time, he reached for the magazine and read the other articles with great interest, particularly the fascinating account of the dinosaurs. But it was Francesca

Mallory's story on the Jews in the little settlement of Clarion that captivated him.

Andre had been all over the world, had probably done more, seen more, than most men he knew. But his education had been seriously neglected in one glaring area. He'd never traveled or worked within the U.S. with the exception of the port cities of New Orleans, New York and L.A.

He had no idea there was such a rich variety of culture within the State of Utah. Her article on the Navajo Indians had him riveted. She always managed to find one of the locals who added the color and history to make the story come alive.

Bemused, he finally turned off the lamp and pounded his pillow into shape. Before succumbing to sleep, the thought crossed his mind that if she'd been along on some of his journeys, she could have made a fortune freelancing for a number of international magazines who would gobble everything she sent in and beg for more.

Tomorrow he needed to get to a drugstore and buy some toiletries. No doubt the latest edition of *Beehive Magazine,* or at least some of the back issues, would be out on the shelves.

She had a rare talent with words and the camera. He couldn't help but be curious to see how she treated the assignment which had sent her to Australia to cover the Tabernacle Choir's trip.

The Hollywood Bowl concert had been exquisite. The music, the words had moved him, disturbed him even. He sensed the same experience had happened to her.

Not for the first time did he reflect on the strange coincidence of their meeting in Los Angeles. His heart had almost failed him when he turned around in his seat and saw her talking to Gerda. Out of nowhere it seemed she'd suddenly made an appearance in the aisle looking a golden-haired vision in a pale blue dress that molded her breathtaking figure…

The first time he'd ever seen her, he'd found her femininity intoxicating. That hadn't changed. In fact, his feelings for her had grown to the point that he realized he had to do something about them. This state of limbo couldn't go on any longer….

* * *

"Frannie?" She heard her voice called over the intercom. "Will you come into my office for a minute please?"

Barney sounded so serious. "Yes, of course. I'll be right there."

As she got to her feet, Paul looked up from his work. "Where are you going? I was just about to read this to you and get your opinion."

"The boss wants to see me."

"Well, don't yak in there too long."

"Yak?"

"That's right. The thing you women do best."

"I'm going to do you a favor and not tell you what you men do best."

"Bless you, my child," He ducked, covering his face with his arms.

Paul was one of the few people who knew her views on men and didn't try to whitewash her concerns. She loved him for it.

"See you in a minute."

She hurried out of her cubicle to the other end of the office. When she tapped on Barney's door, he told her to come in.

"What did yo—" But the rest of her question caught in her throat because Barney had a visitor.

Fran had only felt faint one other time. The night the monk had shown up at the Choir's performance in Los Angeles. She'd never supposed she would see him again.

"Frannie? Are you all right?"

She sank into the nearest chair, her gaze never leaving the monk's. His heavily lashed, dark-brown eyes were far too beautiful to belong to a man.

But then, he was an extremely beautiful man according to the male order of beauty. She'd thought so the first time she had laid eyes on him in the gift shop of the monastery, and more especially now in that wine-dark pullover and tan chinos.

Both articles of clothing molded his whipcord-strong body and powerful thighs. With his olive complexion and the blackness of his hair, he had a slightly European air about him she hadn't noticed before. It made him more intriguing and sophisticated.

He looked dangerous.

A chill of excitement chased across her skin.

"Mr. Benet tells me you two have met not only at the monastery, but in Los Angeles too."

Benet? Was he of French ancestry? It might explain his coloring, but Frenchmen weren't usually that tall, were they?

"That's true, Barney."

When nothing else was forthcoming Barney got that funny look on his face that said he was getting exasperated with her monosyllabic responses. "He wanted to thank you in person for the wonderful article you wrote about Father Ambrose's work at the monastery."

"I couldn't have done it without Mr. Benet's help."

She wondered what explanation, if any, the monk had given Barney about his reasons for being at the monastery when he hadn't presented himself as a monk to her boss.

Still, his spiritual struggle had nothing to do with her. Far be it from Fran to question the deception, or his motives.

The monk sat forward in the chair. "I only gave her a few facts. She turned them into a story every brother is proud of." He may have been talking to Barney, but his eyes never left her face.

"Thank you," she whispered.

Barney ran an agitated hand over his bald spot. He was upset with her, but she couldn't tell him why she was so tongue-tied. She couldn't tell anybody.

"Mr. Benet has also been singing your praises over the cover photo on the September issue. Apparently he knows the German lady in question and has her address. He'd like to send her a copy of the magazine."

"An *autographed* copy, Ms. Mallory," the monk amended. "When Gerda sees herself on the front page and reads about herself in the article on the 'choir of angels' as she calls them, she will think her cup 'runneth over.'"

"I'll be happy to sign one for her."

By now Barney was more or less glaring at her because her natural enthusiasm was missing. He shoved himself away from his desk. "I'll rustle up half a dozen copies for you to sign, Frannie. That way the woman can give them to her family and friends."

As soon as Barney left the room, the monk handed her a copy of the magazine he'd been holding. ‘‘I found this in my room at the monastery last night.’’ He turned to the article on Abbot Ambrose. ‘‘I’d like you to autograph it beneath your name. Please sign it, Francesca, and address it, Dear Andre.’’

Andre. Father Andre Benet. Is that what the brothers called him?

With an unsteady hand, she placed the magazine on Barney’s desk and reached for a pen. In the process, her silken-clad leg accidentally brushed against his knee. She felt as if a bolt of electricity had just charged her body, and quickly moved away from him. If he was aware of the jerky gesture, she didn’t notice because she refused to acknowledge him.

Thankfully Barney reentered the room with a bunch of magazines in hand, breaking the tension crackling around them.

‘‘Is there anything special you’d like me to write to your friends besides my name?’’ She was still seated at the desk, poised to finish the autographing, then leave.

The monk lounged back in the chair with that unconscious masculine grace she’d noticed as they’d walked in the orchard.

"As long as you have six magazines there, make one to Gerda, another to her son, Harbin, another to her grandson, Renke, one to her daughter-in-law Ludwiga, her granddaughter, Adelheide. Oh yes, and Gerda's brother, Kurt."

Fran's mouth tightened. "I'm afraid you'll have to spell all of them for me."

"Of course."

"Would you like a drink, Mr. Benet?" Barney offered. He was being even more affable than usual. "We have coffee, Coke, Seven-Up, ginger ale."

"Nothing for me, thank you, Mr. Kinsale."

"How about you, Frannie?"

"I still have a ginger ale on my desk. Thanks anyway, Barney."

All the time she was signing the magazines, listening for the monk's coaching, she felt his unwavering dark gaze studying her profile and more. Though her sweater and skirt were entirely appropriate, his male scrutiny of her feminine attributes made her feel exposed. With every passing second, she knew the flush on her face had deepened in color.

"There." She lifted her head, bestowing a saccharine smile on Barney. "I've finished. Now if you'll both excuse me, I have a deadline to meet by three o'clock. It was very nice to see you again, Mr. Benet."

She lunged for the door, and practically ran to her desk.

"Good grief. What happened to you?"

She rubbed the back of her neck. "Not now, Paul. I've got a headache coming on."

"He couldn't have fired you."

"No, it's nothing like that."

"He already gave you a raise, so what else is there?"

"You'd be surprised."

"Hey—whatever it is, you're going to live."

"I know. I'll get over it."

I've got to get over it.

Maybe most men in the world were losers. But compared to this monk who had run away from his vows and was living a lie, they were saints!

No matter how attractive he was, Fran hadn't waited twenty-eight years to get mixed up with a tormented monk who'd been cloistered for too long without a woman.

She'd felt his gaze wandering over her just now. It had been far too personal and intimate.

Maybe meeting her at the monastery had caused him to wonder if he really could give up women.

She supposed she should confide in Paul and get his opinion, but he would probably make a joke of it and tell her it was wishful thinking on her part.

Everything would have been all right if she hadn't bumped into the monk in Los Angeles. Now he was back in Salt Lake and had shown up at the office.

A nagging voice told her the whole situation was partially her fault. Because of her attraction to him, she'd gone back to the monastery when it wasn't necessary, and the monk knew it!

She could have sent Paul with the proofs. The monk knew that too!

The other monk who accepted the magazines from her probably did pass her message along. If so, no wonder Mr. Benet, or whoever he really was, felt emboldened enough to seek her out, believing she reciprocated his feelings.

Therein lay her problem. *Part of her did.*

Barney had once told her that she went where angels feared to tread. That was why she made such a good journalist.

Well, this was one time when she wished she had left well enough alone. But that was a lie too, because deep inside she was sick with excitement that he'd come to the office to seek her out.

Heavens— He was back in Salt Lake! *For how long?*

"Frannie?"

She jumped. The sound of her boss's voice over the intercom brought her back to reality in a hurry. She'd only left his office a few minutes ago. Was the monk still there? In panic she turned to Paul.

"Do me a favor and find out if Barney is alone in his office. Don't say anything, just check, and then come back and tell me."

He blinked. "Okay."

It seemed like an eternity before he returned, obviously in a quandary. "What's going on? The boss is upset."

She bit her lip. "Is he alone?"

"The last time I looked."

"Thanks, Paul. I owe you."

"How about an explanation?"

"Maybe later."

"I'm holding you to that."

When she entered Barney's office, he just stared at her without saying anything.

"I know I was awful," she blurted. "But I had my reasons."

"You know what your problem is—you don't like men."

"I like you—and Paul—and Uncle Donald—"

"Don't try to undermine me. I saw exactly what was going on in this room. I felt it. The minute a man gets too close to you, you run the other direction. But this time you've let your fears interfere with your professionalism."

She took a fortifying breath. "Like I said, I had my reasons."

"I'd like to hear them. Sit down."

After doing his bidding she murmured, "I think I'm in trouble."

He looked like he'd been stabbed. "Don't tell me you're going to have his ba—"

"No!" she cried and buried her face in her hands, not knowing whether to laugh or cry. Barney was an upstanding member of his church who came from an era where that expression could only mean one thing. "That isn't the kind of trouble I'm talking about."

"Thank heaven."

"This whole thing started when Paul got sick and asked me to go to the monastery in his place for that story."

For the next little while Barney sat there listening without interrupting. If he was scandalized by her imprudent behavior, he had the good manners not to lecture her.

When she'd told him everything, he sat back in his chair and tapped his reading glasses on the desk. "You're a beautiful woman, Frannie. No man would be immune to you, not even a monk."

"Paul said the same thing."

"That's because it's true."

His comment was unexpected. "Thank you for the compliment, Barney. But you still have to admit it's a bizarre situation."

"You mean a monk who's struggling? He wouldn't be the first man of the cloth to do so, and he certainly won't be the last. You know what I think?"

Her head was bowed. "What?"

"I think you're interested in him. I also think you're shocked at yourself because you've fallen for a mysterious man who seems to be the personification of the very thing that makes you afraid of men."

"I haven't *fallen* for him, Barney."

"Well, that's the term we used to use in my day," he gently mocked. "From where I was sitting, it looked like he was suffering from the same affliction. The truth is, he couldn't take his eyes off of you either."

Naturally Barney noticed everything. "I feel like such a fool."

"Because you've discovered you're vulnerable to a man? Personally I'm glad to see it."

He was beginning to sound like her mother. "I-I'd better get back to work."

"You do that. And if you ever feel like having another chat, you know where to find me."

* * *

In German, Andre wrote:

Dear Gerda—
Out of all the people who attended the choir's concert in Los Angeles, the woman from Beehive Magazine located in Salt Lake City—the woman you talked to after the concert—chose your picture to put on its cover. She used your story in her lead article.

Earlier today I went by her office to get these copies for you and have them signed. I'm sure you and your family will enjoy the articles as much as I have.

Tomorrow I'm leaving for Alaska again and will be gone for an indefinite period. If I can ever be of help to you, for any reason, you can reach me in care of the monastery, #1 Peruvian Drive, Salt Lake City, UT 84999.

Take care until we meet again.

Much love, your friend,

Andre.

Folding the letter on top of the magazines, he sealed the box and handed it to the postal worker. Now he could leave for the airport satisfied that he had repaid Gerda in some small measure for befriending him in Switzerland several years ago at a time when he was at a particularly low ebb.

As for Francesca Mallory, he'd already learned that a trip to the other side of the world couldn't wipe her from his memory. In fact since his first meeting with her, the long stints at sea without being able to see her or hear her voice, had become lessons in self-torture.

Maybe this trip he would finally be able to get her out of his system....

CHAPTER FOUR

FRAN'S PASTOR ALWAYS made it a point to stand in the foyer of the church after services to talk with the members.

She hadn't been to one of his sermons for weeks, probably because she preferred to remain so busy she wouldn't think. Church had a way of making her too introspective. When that happened, all roads led to one man. *Andre Benet.*

There'd been no sign of him since he'd come to her office. She should have rejoiced. Ironically, now that eight weeks had passed without sight or sound of him, that ridiculous longing for him wouldn't go away. If anything, he dominated her every thought, waking or sleeping.

Two feet in front of Fran stood Emily Wilcox who was chatting with the pastor. She was a psychiatrist at University Hospital. For the last few weeks Fran had toyed with the idea of calling her for an appointment. But she hadn't followed through yet.

What would she say to her?

Doctor, I can't let go of this feeling for a celibate monk who thrills and disturbs me at the same time. A man I'll probably never see again. A man struggling with a faith different from my own.

Fran shook her head in self-deprecation. You're a hypocrite, Fran. You don't even profess a strong belief in the faith your mother has espoused and taught you from the cradle.

"It's good to see you, Fran. How are you?"

Her head lifted abruptly. "Pastor Barker—I'm fine. I enjoyed your sermon very much."

"Thank you for those kind words. I'm glad you came. Lucille and I are having an open house for our son, Howard, this evening. We want you to come, anytime after seven."

Fran couldn't help but wonder if Howard was still as crazy about himself as he used to be. She had a feeling her father had started out the same way, a conceited ladies' man. That's why years ago while attending the church's young adult activities and socials, she had kept her distance from the Barkers' son.

Of course Howard had been away at medical school a long time. Maybe the hard knocks of life had made him more bearable. ''Mom told me he's a fully fledged doctor now.''

The Pastor's whole face beamed. ''He is. Nothing could make us happier than knowing he's home to stay.''

''That's wonderful. You must be very proud of him. Naturally I'll drop by.''

Of course becoming a doctor might have made Howard even more arrogant. Wouldn't you know he'd become a woman's doctor?

''Excellent. We'll see you there.''

It was the last thing she wanted to do tonight, but she couldn't be rude. Lately nothing held any particular appeal. It was beginning to worry her.

If it wasn't too late, she would try to catch up with Dr. Wilcox and talk to her. The other woman probably hadn't left the parking lot yet.

But in that assumption Fran was wrong. By the time she'd been forced to stop and talk to a few other people on her way out of the church, Dr. Wilcox's classic green Jaguar with the tan leather seats, which the whole congregation coveted, was nowhere in sight.

Feeling at a loose end, Fran took off in her economy car. There were dozens of things left undone at home, but she was too restless to discipline herself to take care of them. Perhaps a drive that took up a better portion of the day was exactly what she needed.

The family were all having Sunday dinner at her uncle's, but Fran had opted out this time, preferring to be alone. She knew they meant well, but today she couldn't handle the inevitable barrage of questions. If she got hungry, she could eat later at the open house.

The bleak November afternoon fit her mood as she traveled up the canyon to clear her head. With the trees denuded of their leaves, Salt Lake didn't look its most attractive right now. The transformation wouldn't occur until a couple of major snowstorms swept through.

Once again she found herself wishing it were a working day full of so many deadlines she wouldn't have time to think about the monk who—if she were being totally honest with herself—was fast becoming her obsession.

As her car traveled past the turnoff which would eventually lead to the monastery, she increased her speed, refusing to even look in its direction. She wondered if the day would come when she wouldn't be conscious of the monk's existence every time she had to drive past it.

Two hundred miles later, after making the grand loop of several canyons, she ended up on the interstate at the base of the mountains leading south. She was almost out of gas and wouldn't make it back to her apartment without it.

At the turnoff for the freeway, Andre headed north for a mile in his rental car, then took the next exit which brought him to a small shopping center with a couple of restaurants, a minimart and a service station.

He went inside the busy convenience store for a newspaper. Luckily there was one copy of the *Salt Lake Tribune* left in a box. Grateful all the papers hadn't been sold out this late in the day, he got in line to pay for it. That's when he caught sight of a silvery-blonde head. A woman stood several people in front of him. He craned his neck to get a better look.

Instead of flowing to her shoulders, the gossamer hair had been caught back at the crown with a tortoiseshell clip. She was wearing a stunning navy blue suit and matching leather high heels. The collar of the blouse was a lighter blue paisley. From the back she looked elegant, classy, and above all, feminine....

He couldn't wait to see her when she turned around. Judging from their avid stares, neither could the two younger men standing in line ahead of him, discussing her attributes. Absurd as it was, their reaction was making him feel distinctly territorial.

The odds were a million to one, but if she didn't turn out to be Ms. Mallory...

He hadn't wanted to wait until tomorrow to see her, or worse, to find out that she might be out of her office on a story.

Suddenly he caught sight of her profile and couldn't prevent the low groan that escaped. The blood began pounding in his ears.

She started for the doors. He followed, tossing the newspaper back in the box. For a woman in high heels she moved fast. He moved faster. They reached her car at the far gas pump at the same time.

''Francesca?''

Her audible gasp was uniquely satisfying to Andre. It told him among other things that she hadn't forgotten him. More importantly, that she wasn't indifferent to him.

She whirled around, staring at him in unfeigned disbelief. ''What are you doing here?'' she finally blurted.

''I was about to buy a newspaper when I saw you.'' In her dark-fringed eyes, the translucent green color stood out so he couldn't look anywhere else. ''The coincidences seem to keep happening to us.'' Her shallow breathing pleased him no end. ''As soon as I realized it was you, I followed you out of the store.''

When nothing else was forthcoming on her part he added, ''You must admit the odds of our bumping into each other like this aren't as great as they were in Los Angeles. This time I'm only three short miles from the monastery.''

She stared at him so strangely. ''Something tells me you're still afraid my soul is in jeopardy, that I've forsaken my vows.''

The small moan that escaped her lips confirmed his suspicions. A long silence ensued before she said, "You appear to be a restless spirit. It's only natural of me to assume that you still haven't made up your mind whether to stay with the brothers, or leave forever."

"I'm getting closer to a permanent decision."

Her face closed up, intriguing him even more. "I can't imagine being torn in two like that."

"It runs in my family."

"What do you mean?"

"My father had the same problem."

"I still don't understand."

"My father was a monk."

She put a nervous hand to her throat. "Your father?"

"Yes."

"But—" She shook her head. "How could he be?"

"Surely I don't have to explain anything as basic as the attraction between the sexes. It happens, even to celibate monks with the best of intentions. Obviously my mother was a willing participant."

In a quiet voice she said, "I realize that. But it's very sad for a soul to be at war. Is your mother still alive?"

"No."

"Your father?"

"No."

She lowered her eyes. "I'm sorry."

"So am I. From all indications, Abbot Ambrose was a great man."

Fran grasped the car door handle for support as her thoughts flashed back to the magazine photo of the head monk in his younger days.

Abbot Ambrose was Andre Benet's father?

Upon recollection he'd been a very fine-looking man. Now that she knew of his relationship to the arresting male standing in front of her, she wondered why she hadn't noticed the resemblance right away.

Because you were trying so hard not to let this monk figure in your thoughts at all.

She berated herself in disgust because from the first moment they'd met, the memory of him had been haunting her around the clock.

"You talk as if your father were a stranger to you."

"For all intents and purposes, he was. Neither of us had a knowledge of the other until we met for the first time two weeks prior to his death. In fourteen short days we had to make up for a lifetime apart."

She still didn't understand. "Before you met him, were you both monks at different monasteries?"

"Hardly," he mocked.

Fran froze to the spot. "Are you saying you're *not* a monk?"

A subtle smile broke the corner of his mouth. Its masculine curvature did strange things to her insides.

"I wonder if the truth would be any more palatable to you than your own erroneous assumptions about me."

She didn't think she could take much more of this. "If they were erroneous, then you're the one to blame for allowing me to assume something that was patently untrue. There have been several opportunities when you coul—"

"Four to be precise," he interjected before she'd finished speaking. "But I didn't feel the time was right on any of those occasions to correct your thinking.''

''And suddenly now it is?'' Her eyes flashed green fire.

He studied her for a breathless moment. ''Yes. It seems that I haven't been able to get you out of my mind.''

His reluctant admission caused her heart to nearly burst from its chest cavity. ''You mean despite all your efforts?''

''Something like that, yes.''

Fran had no defense against such an admission. With her body trembling, she darted him an icy smile. ''Isn't it fortunate that I'm not suffering from the same dilemma.''

''You know that's not true. So do I,'' came the husky retort. ''If you remember, I was in the same office with you and your boss. He couldn't have helped but be aware of the chemistry between us.''

Terrified because Andre had always been able to feel her attraction to him, she opened the door of her car and got in as fast as she could before closing it. To her consternation, she realized she'd left the car window down, giving him access.

As he lowered his dark head to look in at her, she was unbearably aware of his hands gripping the window sill. "I was going to come by your office tomorrow to ask you out for dinner. But now that you're here in the flesh," came the silky comment, "I find I don't want to wait that long. Spend the rest of the evening with me."

She stared straight ahead. "That would be impossible!"

"Does that mean you're busy?"

"It means I don't accept invitations from virtual strangers."

"We're hardly strangers."

Her head swung around in reaction. It was a mistake. Too late she remembered that she wasn't going to look at him. The banked fire in his eyes excited and frightened her at the same time.

"You are to me," she said, her voice trembling. "Up until now I thought you were a monk!"

The corner of his mouth twitched disturbingly. "A monk with mental problems?" He continued to read her mind with startling accuracy.

"Surely the news that I'm a mere man who finds himself attracted to you should come as a relief. At least now you don't have to feel guilty that all this time you've been tempting a celibate monk beyond his endurance."

Heat scorched her cheeks. His taunt provoked her to cry, "You're wrong, Mr. Benet! If anything your confession makes you more suspect in my eyes than ever. I have no idea who you really are."

"I realize that. Up until now that's the way I've wanted it. You see, Ms. Mallory, over the years I've enjoyed a certain freedom from complications only a woman can cause. Especially a woman like you."

His voice sounded unbearably seductive just now. She gripped the steering wheel tightly. "If that's supposed to be some kind of compliment, it has failed, Mr. Benet. A person who could lie for months about something as fundamental as being a monk, is capable of lying about other things. I want no part of it!"

"If I lied, I did it for my own self-preservation. As long as you believed I was a monk, it made it easier for me to keep my distance from you. Or so I thought..." he added on a note of self-mockery.

"However, contrary to what you're thinking, I didn't start out with the intention of lying to you. When you came to the monastery, my father was on the verge of death. I didn't want the others waiting on him. I hugged that privilege for myself." Fran could hear the love in his voice as he talked about his parent.

"We decided I should dress like the brothers to avoid speculation on thc part of any visitors who might see me coming and going. On the morning of your arrival, I'd been up all night holding him so he could breathe more easily."

Dear God. It explained so much about that day. Tears sprang to her eyes.

"We argued about his giving your magazine the interview at all. He was far too frail. But he insisted that it was important to him, so I told him I would handle the initial meeting in his place."

She sat there spellbound, all the while feeling his dark gaze wander over her profile.

"When you came into the gift shop, you seemed to bring the essence of that spring day with you. Suddenly I resented your energy, your ability to get on about your business while the father I barely knew lay dying in a cell-like room.

"Because of the precariousness of his situation, I resented the intrusion which took me away from his bedside. More, I resented the fact that despite my pain, I felt an unwanted attraction to you.

"The second time you came to the monastery, I was in deep pain over my father's death. Yet my attraction to you appeared to be stronger than ever. I wondered what it was about you that could get beneath my skin even when I had reached the lowest point of my life.

"None of it made sense. Of course I didn't want it to make sense. I didn't want to feel an attachment to you. Commitment was something I had always avoided, so I perpetuated the myth that I was a monk and purposely chose to forget you.

"But destiny seems to have had other plans for us. When we met at the concert, I realized I was in trouble where you were concerned. That night I came close to telling you the truth. But a part of me was still angry that I couldn't get you out of my mind.

"I'll be honest with you, Francesca. I've known several women in my life intimately, but in the end, I never felt anything lasting. Then I met you." His voice grated. "The attraction was immediate and has never gone away. At this point I want to explore what there could be between us because I know you feel that attraction too."

She felt a delicious shiver chase across her skin.

"You know I'm the son of Father Ambrose," he persisted with unflappable calm. "Correct me if I'm wrong, but I believe you entitled your story on him, 'Monument to a Saint.' Surely that's a starting place for us. By the time we finish our meal, we'll both know a great deal more about each other. It's long past time, don't you agree?"

The temptation to say yes was overpowering. But his honesty had created new demons. His admission that he hadn't been able to stay in one relationship with a woman terrified her.

He didn't sound that different from her own father who stopped loving her mother and moved on. Fran wasn't about to repeat history.

"I appreciate your honesty, and I admit there's an attraction. But I can't go out with you, Andre—" she blurted without looking at him. "Don't ask me why, I just can't. Now if you'll excuse me, I'm late for an open house."

There was a tension-filled silence. "I envy you," he murmured.

"What do you mean?" His comment had thrown her off base once more.

"You have someplace to go, people to see who care about you. I'm not from Salt Lake. Because I'm the son of the deceased Abbot, I've been treated as a special guest at the monastery. But I can't take advantage of their hospitality forever, and the monks aren't allowed to fraternize. As it stands, I don't know a single soul in the city except *you*."

He sounded lonely. *Damn him.*

She took a shuddering breath. "If you're trying to make me feel sorry for you, it won't work."

"You misunderstand me. I thought I was making it clear that you're the only reason I'm in Salt Lake at all."

"I'm sorry for you then, because I couldn't possibly consider having a serious relationship with you,'' she said to cover her pounding heart.

''If that's true, why did Brother Joseph tell me how disappointed you were when you came to the monastery with the magazines and discovered I was no longer there?''

Her face went hot. ''He must have imagined it.''

''No. He distinctly said you were upset, and wanted to know where I'd gone. That doesn't sound like a woman who couldn't possibly considering having a relationship with me.''

''Please, Andre—'' she cried in protest. She was sinking fast.

''Please what? Do you suppose I'm just imagining thc wild throbbing at the base of your throat not covered by that attractive blouse you have on? Everything you wear suits your remarkable coloring and figure.''

Floundering she said, ''T-That was too personal a remark to make to someone you scarcely know.''

''In May we shared an interesting hour putting ideas for your magazine together, but it wasn't long enough. Neither was our too-brief meeting in Los Angeles. That's why I'm back, to remedy the situation. But if you take strong offense to a simple compliment from me, then I guess I don't need to wonder how you'll react to *this.*''

She glimpsed a look of raw desire in his eyes before he caught her face between his hands. They felt strong and male against her skin.

He was going to kiss her right in front of everyone coming in and out of the convenience store!

Before she could let out a cry of protest, his mouth covered hers, smothering the sound. She tried to fight him, but there was no place to go.

With relentless precision he forced her against the headrest, coaxing her lips apart until the two of them were moving and breathing as one flesh.

Unbelievably, she found herself kissing him back, one kiss after another until she lost count in her feverish need to prolong this overwhelming feeling of rapture.

Until this moment she'd never known the meaning of ecstasy. The world started to spin out of control. To her shock, the small moaning noises she could hear were coming from her own throat.

She couldn't get close enough to him. Something was preventing her from molding herself to his hard, powerful body. As she yearned toward him, her knees came up against the closed door. That's when she realized the extent of her euphoria. Their involvement had caused her to lose cognizance of time and place.

Too soon he relinquished her swollen lips with a satisfied smile. "Don't ever tell me again you're not interested." His husky whisper resonated to her insides. "Enjoy the open house."

"Fran! How nice you came. Howard has been asking about you. Go on in the dining room. Mrs. Landers is telling him all about her ailments. I think he could use rescuing," the pastor said with a twinkle in his light gray eyes.

She smiled like an automaton and followed the other late arrivals headed for the food. She couldn't believe she was able to walk upright and chat about inconsequential matters as if nothing had happened to her.

Surely everyone in the Barker home could tell she'd been kissed senseless. One look in the rearview mirror had confirmed her suspicions. Her eyes held an abnormal glow. The reddened skin around her mouth was still tender to the touch from his five o'clock shadow. Her pulse rate had tripled. Worst of all, whenever she remembered his mouth on hers, her body ached with an indescribable pain.

All her life she'd heard about that magical thing called "chemistry." She knew it had to exist, otherwise there would be no drive to perpetuate the species.

But nothing could have prepared her for the life-changing experience which had just taken place inside her car with a man who was more of a stranger to her than ever.

Before tonight, she had imagined him lodged with his brothers. She'd envisioned him being in that setting since his late teens when many young men decided to join the priesthood, an environment she could picture as a place of safety and refuge.

To find out he had no religious vocation meant that all his adult years he'd been other places doing other things, which made him more of a mystery than ever.

He was a man of the world.

Naturally there'd been other women. No man as attractive as Andre Benet would have reached his midthirties without getting involved. But by his own admission, none of his affairs had lasted.

That's what they were. *Affairs.* Just like her father.

The fact that she still knew nothing about his home or the way he earned his living, made what she'd done with him in the car so much worse. To her shame, she had returned his kisses with torrid intensity. Nothing like this had ever happened to her before.

She didn't even want to think about the women who'd been intimately involved with him. No doubt his sex appeal was too potent for a woman to resist.

Fran was a case in point!

But even if she hungered to be in his arms again, to be thrilled by the taste and feel of his mouth, the thought of getting involved with a man who admitted he'd always been a free spirit was out of the question.

If and when the day came that she were truly to fall in love, it would have to be with an honorable man of integrity who wanted to put down roots, someone with a solid background and values.

"Five dollars for those troubling thoughts," a male voice said, jolting her back to the present.

She lifted her head. "Howard—"

"You remembered my name. That's something at least."

His clear blue eyes hadn't changed. They still looked at her with the same male admiration she remembered, but they were also asking questions.

No doubt he would make a fine obstetrician. Without saying a word, he sensed she was tortured about something and had invited her to confide in him. Under other circumstances she might have found herself telling him her problems, just like Mrs. Landers.

"Your thoughts still have you tongue-tied," he murmured with a trace of compassion. "I can't believe you're not married with a couple of children by now."

"I was going to say the same thing about you. As for me, I've been too busy establishing my own career."

"I know. Dad showed me the issue of *Beehive Magazine* with your story on the Tabernacle Choir making the cover page. Congratulations! You're a very gifted writer and photographer."

"Thank you. You haven't done so badly yourself, *Doctor.* Though I feel I should apologize for your father. I know he's always interested in everyone who makes up his congregation, but I'm sure you could have done without the magazine being thrust in your face."

He smiled his old smile, but the arrogance was missing. The handsome, blond six-foot teenager who'd been two years older than herself had turned into an even better-looking, darker-blond man of thirty.

"On the contrary. I asked him to keep me posted about you."

Fran had no idea. Not after all these years.

"Then let me be one in a long line of people to say, welcome home."

A faint smile broke the corner of his mouth. "You sound like you meant that."

The directness of his comment puzzled her. "Of course I did. I do! Everyone is proud of the local boy who made good, particularly your parents."

One brow quirked. "Does this mean you would finally consider going out on a date with me? I've been waiting nine years for the opportunity."

Fran would have laughed if any other male acquaintance from her past had made a remark like that. But because this was Howard, and she was aware of how she had rebuffed him quite mercilessly when they were teenagers, she experienced a healthy dose of remorse.

In truth, he'd never done anything wrong. Because of her bitterness over her adulterous father's multiple affairs, she had made the pastor's attractive son an unwitting target, painting him and her unfaithful parent with the same brush.

"If you're asking, then I accept."

He shook his head. "Just like that. Incredible. How about tomorrow night? We could go to dinner as soon as I finish my hospital rounds.''

Howard was exactly what she needed right now to put thoughts of Andre Benet away for good.

''Tomorrow night would be perfect. What time?''

''Can I call you?''

''Do you have my number?''

''I have the latest church directory.''

''It's in there. I'll look forward to seeing you.'' She turned to go.

''Surely you're not leaving the open house yet. You haven't tasted my mother's chicken-and-broccoli casserole.'' Nothing seemed to have escaped Howard's notice. But she'd lost her appetite after her encounter with the monk.

No, not a monk. He wasn't a man of the cloth. She didn't know who he was.

Pausing midstride she said, ''I've been out of town most of the day and I have a dozen things to do before work in the morning. Do you mind if I duck out?''

His eyes narrowed on her features, almost as if he knew she was hiding a guilty secret from the world.

"Of course not. I should consider myself lucky you came by the house at all. I'll call you tomorrow either at your work or your apartment."

He had definitely grown up.

The younger man would have pressed her to stay until he'd forced her to say something cutting so he would stop. This new mature version was willing to bide his time.

"Thank you. Good night, Howard."

"Thank *you,* Fran. Good night."

It was dark out and growing colder. Because of the crowd at the Barker house, she'd had to park a block down the street. Anxious to get home and try to come to terms with what happened to her earlier in the evening, she hurried toward her car. Before she reached it, she saw something white which had been placed beneath her windshield wiper.

At first she thought it must be an ad. But one look at all the other cars and she realized the envelope had been put there on purpose for her.

With her heart in her throat she grabbed it, then got in her car. Once inside, she locked the doors before turning on the map light to read the contents.

Her hands were shaking so badly, she couldn't hold the note steady.

In bold, beautiful cursive writing it read:

Francesca,
I didn't follow you to frighten you. Since I don't know where you live, and I have no desire to upset you by phoning your office or showing up there again without an invitation, I was left with no other alternative than this one.

By the time you read my note, I'll be back at the monastery waiting for you to come. The chapel doors will be left open until midnight. We need to talk. If you don't come, then I'll know the feelings I experienced while I was kissing you a while ago were all on my part, and I won't bother you again.

Andre.

Fran's mouth went dry as sawdust. She read the note a dozen times before crushing it in her palm.

Andre Benet knew exactly what he was doing. No matter how many unanswered questions she had about him, he realized her greatest fear was of her own unbridled response to the passion he'd brought to life inside her.

She didn't have to be a prophetess to know that if she drove to the monastery tonight, they wouldn't stay in the chapel to talk.

With her body still on fire for him, his note tempted her to do something she could never have imagined doing before she met him. But if she obeyed that desire, something told her she would live to regret it forever.

Tonight Howard had asked her to go out with him. Because he was a thoroughly nice person, and because she felt guilty over her treatment of him years ago, she had decided to accept his invitation for dinner.

What kind of a woman would she be if she could make a date with a man whose family she'd known for years, only to run back to the arms of a footloose, enigmatic stranger whose past she knew nothing about in order to experience his lovemaking the second she was out of Howard's sight?

You'd be the female version of your father.

Horrified by the answer, Fran started up the car and headed for her apartment as if demons were in pursuit.

CHAPTER FIVE

ANDRE KNEW FRANCESCA wanted to come. She couldn't have responded to him the way she had unless she'd wanted him as much as he'd wanted her. That explosion of need wasn't something either of them would be able to forget.

But even as he'd penned his note, he knew in his heart of hearts she wouldn't come tonight. She wasn't ready to admit the depth of her feelings for him yet.

Still, he intended to wait until midnight, and sat down on the stone bench outside the monastery to catch up on his correspondence. Beneath the exterior wall lamp he read the latest letter from Gerda.

Dear Andre

Your package arrived like a gift from heaven. I could not stop crying. I thank you from the bottom of my heart.

I would also like to thank the beautiful

young journalist. Maybe one day soon I'll be able to do that in person.

As you know when we all met in Los Angeles to attend the concert together, Harbin had just finished up interviews for a teaching position in the States.

Well, we have now heard back with wonderful news. He was offered professorships at UCLA, The University of Washington, and the University of Utah. The best news is, he has decided to accept the position of associate professor of German at the University of Utah.

So we are moving to Salt Lake for good! Since I first heard the Tabernacle Choir sing, I have always wanted to live there.

We are at this minute packing up our house in Zurich, and making preparations to come by the first of December. We won't be able to look for a place to live until we arrive there, but I don't mind. My prayers have been answered. God has been so good to me and my family, I could never complain about anything.

Andre, *mein schatz,* you do realize that

once we are settled, you will always have a standing invitation to stay with us whenever you pass through Salt Lake to visit your father's grave. Our home is your home. You know that.

I'll talk to you again soon. Take care of yourself.

With much love,

Gerda.

He shook his head incredulously. Gerda and her family were going to make a home in Salt Lake of all places. Who would ever have dreamed it?

Of course the news was as delightful to him as it was unexpected.

He pocketed her letter and pulled out the newspaper. After following Francesca to her party, he'd purchased one at another convenience store. With an eagerness abetted by a surge of pure adrenaline, he turned to the real estate section.

At one minute past twelve, he folded the paper beneath his arm and went inside to turn out lights and lock up. Before long he would find himself a place to live.

Nothing would give him greater pleasure than to invite Gerda and her family to stay with *him.* After they'd opened their home to him while he'd been a student in Zurich, he could finally return the favor.

But that only gave him a month to buy the right house in the right neighborhood and get it furnished in time for guests. It meant he would have to work fast if all his plans for the future were going to materialize.

Howard insisted on walking Fran to the front door of her apartment in the lighted twelve-unit complex. She could tell from the way he was looking at her that he didn't want the evening to end. Fran, on the other hand, was still in too much turmoil over Andre Benet to know how she felt about anything.

"Thank you for a wonderful dinner, Howard. I really enjoyed it."

"So did I. How would you like to attend the opera with me next Friday night? They're putting on 'The Marriage of Figaro.'"

"If I weren't going to be out of town, I'd love it."

His brows came together. ‘‘A magazine assignment?’’

‘‘Yes. I’m doing an article on the West Desert which includes covering the car races at the Bonneville Salt Flats.’’

‘‘That means you’ll be spending the night in Wendover.’’

She could tell where his thoughts were headed. Not wanting to give him the chance to ask if he could join her she said, ‘‘Actually I’m camping out at Blue Lake with friends. You remember Sylvia Wherett?’’

‘‘Vaguely.’’

‘‘Sylvia remembers you. I happen to know she had a huge crush on you in high school. All the girls did.’’

There was no answering smile. ‘‘I didn’t notice.’’

Once again Fran had said the wrong thing. Every time she tried to keep things light, his response tended to put a damper on the conversation.

‘‘Well, that was a long time ago. She’s married now. Fred, her husband, is a diving master who teaches scuba diving for the University of Utah. She’s in his class. The students are driving out there this weekend to certify. I'm going to take some pictures and do a few interviews as part of my article. I don't think I'll be home until late Sunday night.''

He eyed her through veiled eyes. ''Was this a token date, Fran? My parents forced you to come to the open house, and you felt you had no choice but to take pity on me?''

''No,'' she protested. ''I swear that's not the case.''

''Then there's someone else, and the two of you are in the middle of an argument.''

She shook her head. ''You're wrong, Howard. I haven't dated in months.'' The unexpected encounters with Andre were something else....

''That doesn't mean a thing if your emotions are involved elsewhere,'' he persisted. ''I've been around the block a few times. Believe me, I know when my date is with me or not. Tonight I had dinner with a lovely facsimile of Fran Mallory, but the real woman was nowhere to be found.''

She averted her eyes. ''I'm sorry. You're the last person in the world I would want to offend.''

"I believe you. So tell me what's really going on with you. Are you in love with this man?"

"I told you," she insisted, her voice throbbing, "it's not like that."

"Then what *is* it like?"

"I'd rather not talk about it."

He let out a defeated sigh. "Time hasn't changed you. You're still fighting your own nature."

Her head lifted "What do you mean?"

"Your father did a lot of damage. Have you considered counseling?"

She might have resented the question if it had been asked by anyone but Howard.

An image of Dr. Wilcox flashed through her mind. "Actually I have."

"Then it would be a step in the right direction. The fact is, I'd like to get to know you a good deal better, but that's never going to happen until you've worked through your distrust of men and learn to risk loving again. Good night, Fran."

He was down the steps before she could think to call out to him. "Howard? Please don't leave here upset. May I phone you next week?''

After a brief silence, ''Only if you mean it.''

He had just put her on notice that he was not a man to be trifled with. She would have to know her own mind before she tried to contact him again.

Long after she'd let herself inside the apartment and had gone to bed, Fran lay there wide awake pondering his remarks. Other people—her mother, Barney, Paul—had told her the same thing. But hearing it from Howard brought it down to a much more personal level.

He wasn't only a medical doctor giving expert advice—he was a very attractive, intelligent, decent, eligible man who had everything to offer a woman. There was no doubt in Fran's mind he would make a wonderful husband. She should be flattered that he wanted to get to know her better. She *was* flattered.

More than that, she admired him for not being willing to put up with a twenty-eight-year-old woman who should have done something about her emotional hang-ups long before now.

If she could get past them, then she could explore what might be between her and Howard. But before she dared approach him, she needed to get Andre Benet out of her system.

Fran turned over on her stomach and hugged the pillow like a lifeline. What a coward she'd been to run away from him on Sunday. It proved how dysfunctional she really was.

If she had just accepted his invitation to spend the rest of the evening with him, she wouldn't be in such torment now. Her unwillingness to meet him halfway had provoked him into kissing her.

She had no doubt that part of her overwhelming physical response to his lovemaking stemmed from the fact that he represented the proverbial forbidden fruit. Take away the mystery and she could view him like she did any other man of her acquaintance.

Who was it who said there was no greater fear than fear itself?

Andre hadn't done anything so horrible. Following her to the Barker's house to put a note on her car hadn't constituted a crime. *He wasn't a monk, and never had been!*

That was her problem. Her mind persisted in thinking of him in that light. It was his fault for perpetuating the lie for so long. But he'd also explained his reasons for keeping the truth from her, reasons which threw her into another kind of turmoil she didn't want to think about.

Nevertheless, she now knew Andre was an eligible male. Naturally he'd responded like one. It was Fran who'd behaved abnormally. The first time she'd gone out to the monastery had been a favor to Paul. But after that she could have asked someone else on staff to finish up the assignment.

Instead, she'd bought a new dress and had entered the gift shop like a lovesick schoolgirl frantic to talk to the object of her desire. She had no right to blame him for pursuing her. If anything she'd been the one to initiate her present predicament.

No one needed to tell her that if she stayed on this track, she might end up a bitter old woman Until now she hadn't really cared. But seeing Howard again after all these years reminded her how long she'd been angry with her father.

Without knowing the details, Howard had zeroed in on her problem and had given her a real wake-up call. Maybe he was right, and she'd allowed the hurt to canker her soul to the point that she was incapable of trusting any man. It was an ugly indictment, one she thought about the rest of the night.

When morning came, she phoned the office to inform them she'd be in late. Then she got ready and headed for the monastery.

No doubt Andre would be surprised to see her. But since her private phone and address were unlisted, and since he'd made it clear he wouldn't bother her at the office without an invitation first, she realized it was up to her if they were ever to see each other again.

For her peace of mind she needed to talk to him one more time. He was no longer a mystery to her. She could view him the same way she viewed any man she met in the everyday course of her work.

He would say A, and she would say B. By the end of their conversation, she would have no more curiosity about him than she would someone like Paul. At that point she'd be able to walk away and move on to Howard without any ghosts between them. Fran recognized that Howard Barker was the kind of man you *married.*

If she hadn't allowed her father's sins to cripple her, who knows what might have happened between her and the pastor's son years earlier. She owed it to herself to find out because Howard had made it clear he wouldn't wait around forever.

It was a typical winter morning, overcast and freezing cold. Snow from the last storm covered the grounds and roof of the monastery. As she made her away along the private drive, she noticed an elegant, state-of-the-art, midnight-blue Mercedes sedan coming toward her from the direction of the monastery.

She slowed down and pulled to the far right, to allow the other car to pass. To her surprise, the Mercedes came to a full stop when it reached her. Curiosity prompted her to gaze at the unsmiling, black-haired male at the wheel.

Andre.

The world stood still.

He looked…wonderful. In a black turtleneck sweater, there was no other word to describe his dark, virile appeal.

His eyes played over her hair and face, but no words passed his lips. He wasn't about to make this easy for her. She deserved that.

But during the night, when she'd thought about her plan to confront him, it had been in theory only. Seeing him in the flesh wasn't supposed to make her heart leap like this.

"G-Good morning," she stammered, feeling as awkward as a schoolgirl.

As his eyes narrowed on her mouth, she was reminded of Sunday evening when he'd kissed them both into oblivion. She could hardly breathe.

In a gush of words she said, "I came to see you, but it appears you have other plans so—"

"Drive your car to the parking area and I'll follow," he cut in before she could finish.

Her body, particularly her legs, shook so hard she didn't know if she could function well enough to put her economy car in gear and travel the short distance to the monastery. But by some miracle she made it to her destination.

Before she'd turned off the ignition, he'd pulled up next to her and was out of his car. With each step that brought him closer, her pulse accelerated.

Determined not to be a captive audience again, she hurriedly got out to face him on an equal footing. But that was a mistake because he stood too close to her. With his hands on his hips, he looked incredibly masculine. She couldn't help but notice the way his jeans molded his powerful thighs, emanating a soul-destroying sensuality. Fran felt it in every atom of her body.

''Have you taken the day off from work?''

''No. I phoned in and told them I'd be there later.''

His gaze made an intimate sweep of her face and jacket-clad figure. ''How much later?''

She bit her lip. ''For as long as it took to talk to you. That is, presuming I could find you.''

''Evidently you prefer seven-thirty in the morning to the last stroke of midnight,'' he murmured dryly, causing her to blush. ''Have you had breakfast?''

"No." Anticipating a meeting with him had robbed her of an appetite. Before she left her apartment she couldn't have eaten anything if her life had depended on it.

"Neither have I. There's a coffee shop about two miles north of here called the Copper Kettle."

"I've been there many times."

"Good. We could go in my car. But if you're afraid I'll carry you off to some place where no one will ever be able to trace us, then I'll be happy to meet you there."

"Andre—" she murmured with a mixture of guilt and exasperation.

"Be careful what you say. It isn't as if I haven't thought about it."

His warning, delivered in that deep, grating voice, sounded serious enough to send prickles of awareness through her quivering frame.

Sucking in her breath she said, "It would be foolish to take two cars."

"I agree. Yours or mine?"

He was still giving her the chance to stay in control, but none of it mattered because no matter what she chose, he knew she felt totally out of control around him.

"I have to confess I wouldn't mind driving there in your rental car."

The look of satisfaction in his eyes almost made her change her mind. But if she ran away now, it would be admitting defeat. For her ultimate good, she had to follow through with her plan.

"Be sure to lock your car. These days a monastery parking lot is as unsafe as any other."

"You're right."

Grateful that he had reminded her, she turned away from him long enough to press the remote car lock on her key chain. When she heard the click, she walked around to the passenger side of the Mercedes where he held the door open for her.

This time she was careful to make certain the skirt of her sage-colored, brushed-suede suit didn't ride up her legs like before. But when she felt his black gaze wander over her hair, she realized that she needn't have worried about exposing too much nylon-clad thigh.

"This car looks and smells brand-new," she said after he'd gone around and had levered himself into the driver's seat.

He shut the door, then turned his head and flashed her a penetrating glance. ‘‘I bought it off the dealership lot yesterday.’’

Like all precision-made German cars, the Mercedes purred quietly when he turned on the ignition.

‘‘Are you planning to drive this back to New Orleans?’’

‘‘Why would I be going there?’’ he plied in a level voice as they started down the winding drive.

‘‘Isn’t it your home?’’

‘‘Where would you get an idea like that?’’

She blinked. ‘‘I guess I assumed it because of the information you gave me about your father for the magazine article.’’

‘‘I was born there,’’ he admitted, sounding far away, ‘‘but it was never home to me. The day I turned seventeen, I left and went to sea.’’

To sea?

Her mind raced on as she imagined him looking heartbreakingly handsome in full dress uniform. ‘‘Are you in the Navy then? Is that why you come and go at periodic intervals?’’

‘‘Nothing so romantic,’’ he muttered in a harsh tone, reading her mind with embarrassing ease. "I've traveled the world many times over as a merchant seaman."

Merchant seaman?

Her breath caught in her throat. Just the word "seaman" conjured up images of a man with no home, no ties. A restless soul who couldn't stand to be in port very long before he moved on to somewhere else. *To someone else.*

"Have you heard enough?"

"No!" she denied swiftly, looking anywhere except at him. "O-Of course not."

"Then what am I to make of that horrified expression on your face?"

"I'm not horrified," she said defensively.

"The hell you're not!"

In the next breath he made a U-turn on the quiet street leading to the freeway and headed back in the direction of the monastery.

"What are you doing?"

"Taking you to your car, of course."

"No, Andre!" she cried in alarm, unconsciously putting a hand on his arm to stop him. With a sense of wonder she felt his body tauten before he suddenly floored the accelerator and drove the remaining distance in a sinfully short amount of time. After drawing alongside her car, he turned to her.

"You were right not to come to the chapel last night. You're playing with fire. Get out of the car now, Francesca, while I'm still in the mood to let you go. Run back to your own kind."

She struggled for breath. "What do you mean?"

"Exactly what I said."

His expression looked like thunder. The way his hands gripped the steering wheel, she could tell he was barely holding on to his control. It caused her temper to flare.

"Why are you deliberately trying to frighten me off? I'll admit I'm surprised at the way you've earned your living all these years, b-but—"

"You mean shocked!" he broke in. "Right now you're wondering how I could be the son of a monk who anchored himself to one spot for the whole of his adult life.

"I asked myself the same question when I learned my father was still alive. An abbot, no less, of a monastery tucked away in some god-forsaken desert city. Until that moment, Salt

Lake represented nothing more than an inconsequential dot on a map of a place I'd never seen, nor had the slightest desire to visit.''

The raw emotion in his voice caught at her heartstrings. ''Who told you he was alive?''

''My Aunt Maudelle.''

''Not your own mother?'' she questioned before she realized how judgmental that sounded.

''Perhaps she would have told me one day if she hadn't died giving birth to me.''

Aghast, Fran stared at him, unable to look away. She hadn't known about his mother.

To find out he'd lost her at birth, and then found his own father just two short weeks before losing him forever? She couldn't comprehend what a shock that must have been to him.

It explained more than ever his hostile behavior toward her when she first met him at the monastery. He'd been in excruciating pain. No wonder he'd guarded those few precious hours he had left with his father for himself. The last thing he would have wanted was to deal with a journalist who didn't know how to take no for an answer.

Her conscience smote her again as she recalled how shamelessly she'd baited him because of her compelling attraction to him.

"It seems cruel that your aunt waited so long before she told you he was alive." At least Andre could be proud of *his* father, and deserved to have had more time with him.

"She never married or had children of her own. With hindsight I believe she worried that if I learned her secret, I wouldn't love her anymore. It wasn't true of course. I loved her very much.

"I sent her money and made visits to Louisiana to see her. But it wasn't until she was on her deathbed that her conscience finally got the best of her."

Another loss for him. Fran was devastated by everything he'd told her.

"So now you understand that my life has not been a conventional one. Until recently, all those years at sea have suited me perfectly well. It's good, hard, honest work that has provided me adventure and a viable income. But I'm aware not all women would find much to recommend it, particularly not a woman like you."

His piercing gaze saw more than he knew, but she didn't want to go down that precarious path.

"So now that we have my history out of the way, let's talk about what's going on inside you, Francesca. Why have you suddenly chosen this moment in time to offer yourself as the sacrificial lamb at my altar?"

Desperate to keep the situation from exploding she said in a breathless voice, "I drove over here this morning b-because someone important made me realize I needed to deal with my insecurities."

"Someone important?" he prodded mercilessly.

"Yes."

"A man?"

"Yes," she whispered.

"He's threatened by me?"

"Look, Andre—" she explained jerkily because he had hit on the truth "—I ran away from you on Sunday. It was immature of me. I thought if I came over here this morning we could have a n-normal conversation like two sensible adults, then—"

"Then I would go away like a nice little boy and leave you to your sheltered existence with a man who has the right pedigree and credentials? A man who's *safe?*" He bit out an expletive. "If so, let me destroy that myth once and for all.

"I'm a man who happens to desire you in all the ways a man can desire a woman. If you were honest, you would admit that your presence here this morning tells me you feel exactly the same way about me. Since nothing about our relationship has been normal from the beginning, I think you already know it's past time for total honesty here."

With his dark eyes searching hers, he moved closer, putting his arm behind her seat. "Why don't you start by telling me what man put the fear in you in the first place."

Ensnared by too many emotions, she blurted that it was her father.

"What exactly did he do?"

"What most men do to their wives," she answered, her voice wobbling precariously.

After a pause, "In other words, he was unfaithful."

"Yes."

"When did you first learn about it?"

"I was seven. One day I ran in the house after playing with my friends and saw my mother in the living room sobbing. When I asked her what was wrong, she told me my father had gone away. Since he was out of town on business most of the time, I didn't understand what she meant.

"That's when she explained to me that some men get very restless and can't stay in one place very long. No one knows why. They just can't be tied down.

"She said that he'd had many girlfriends over the years and had finally gone off with one of them.

"At the time I was too young to comprehend what she'd told me. I loved my father. All I worried about was when he was coming home. She said she didn't think he'd be back." Fran stopped to clear her throat. "Her words were prophetic. I never saw him again."

A grimace marred his features before he withdrew his arm and sat back in the seat.

"I'm sorry you've had to live with so much pain. The only difference between your father and myself is that throughout my travels around the world, I was never interested in any woman enough to marry her and have children.

"It took great courage for you to come here today.

After the strange history we've shared, let alone the things I've just told you about myself, you have every right to believe your life has been twice star-crossed.

"Now that our normal conversation between two sensible adults has come to its conclusion, go back to that important man and assure him he has nothing to worry about."

She sat frozen to the seat. After achieving what she'd set out to accomplish, she found she wasn't prepared for things to end this abruptly.

"Andre—"

"For the love of God— A man can only take so much. You know as well as I do what will happen if we spend any more time together. Aside from everything else, somewhere deep in my gut I have this feeling you've never been intimate with a man."

Fran stirred restlessly, unable to look at him.

"I knew I was right," he gasped. "Either get in your own car now, or I won't be responsible for the consequences."

She reached for the door handle, but couldn't bring herself to open it. Not while she was grappling with so many revelations on top of her chaotic emotions.

"W-Where will you go when you leave the monastery?" she cried in a panic-stricken voice.

His sharp intake of breath sounded like ripping silk. It brought her head back around. He darted her an enigmatic glance. "Why do you want to know? Of what possible interest could it be to you?"

On the night of the open house, he'd told her the only reason he'd come back to Salt Lake was because of her. The idea of never seeing him again was anathema to her.

Her hand curled into a fist. "Please, Andre."

"Please what?" he demanded.

She swallowed hard. "Will you ever come back to the monastery?"

After a heart-pounding pause he said, "Not to stay. But there will be times when I'll want to visit my father's grave. If by chance you and I should cross paths again, you can consider it another astounding coincidence. Goodbye, Francesca.''

He meant for her to get out of the car on her own.

With clumsy, wooden movements, she finally did his bidding. But even before she heard the door close, the Mercedes was moving away from her.

She watched until it disappeared around the first bend in the drive. At that point a searing pain pierced her heart. She had the awful premonition that she'd just let go of something vital to her existence.

Terrified this might be a permanent condition, she got in her car and started driving. By the time she reached the mouth of Parley's Canyon, she heard a siren. When she looked in her rearview mirror she realized a police car had been pursuing her. In her agony, she never noticed he'd been trying to get her to pull over.

It was her first speeding ticket since high school. Normally the incident would have upset her. But her pain over saying goodbye to

Andre was so acute, the citation and warning meant less than nothing to her.

By the time she reached Heber thirty-six miles away, she realized that running away wouldn't make the pain disappear. Nothing but a miracle could accomplish that feat. The temporary panacea was to go back to the office and work until she dropped from exhaustion.

But as she was to find out in the days ahead, no amount of extra work for the magazine or outings with friends, let alone the Thanksgiving holiday with her family, provided surcease from the continual ache in her heart.

She purposely avoided church because she knew Howard would be there. Until the worst of the pain faded, she didn't want to suffer from guilt as well.

How right Howard had been when he'd told her a person didn't have to be in a relationship to feel emotionally involved with another person.

She'd never been out on a date with Andre. Aside from the initial interview in order to write her article, they'd only seen each other a few times in passing. For several stolen moments she'd known the primitive fire of his kiss, and had responded with a fierce hunger of her own. That was all....

Fran kept asking herself how three small hours spent in total with this man since last April could have had such a lasting effect on her.

What did it mean when she knew he was the kind of man whose rootless lifestyle could break a woman's heart into tiny bits? No doubt there were bits of his ex-lovers' hearts strewn all over the earth. If that was the case, then why did his image continue to press in on her thoughts?

Her nights were the worst. Tormented by memories of the way it felt to be in his arms, she hadn't had a good sleep in months. If this was love, and she was very much afraid that it was, then she wondered how long her torment would last.

There was an old adage about love having to be fed.

Maybe if she were starved long enough by Andre's absence, her love would eventually wither and die.

CHAPTER SIX

"GERDA? NOW THAT your family has settled in with me, I thought we could give a joint housewarming-Christmas party. I know there are people you want to invite. It would provide me the perfect opportunity to thank my neighbors and a few business people who've made me feel right at home."

"I would love it!" She clapped her hands. "But only if you will let me do the cooking and the decorating."

Andre smiled with satisfaction. "I was hoping you would say that. I have a passion for your fine German cooking left over from my university days in Zurich. My mouth's been watering for homemade *Wiener schnitzel* and Christmas *kuchen.*"

"My mouth is watering for them too! This will be wonderful!"

"While you're with me, this is your home. Do exactly as you would do back in Switzerland."

Her eyes lit up. "I brought all my decorations with me, but they are in storage."

"We'll get them out tomorrow. Right now I'm printing up the invitations and envelopes. I checked with Harbin and we thought next Saturday night would be a good time for the party. Mid-December, people can still find the time to come. He gave me the names and addresses of some people from the university. What about your list?"

"Well—I think it would be nice to invite the Bishop and his counselors from the church here who have been in touch with me all this time. And their families, of course. And there's that nice man and his wife who sang in the choir, the people we met at dinner that night in Zurich after the performance."

"I remember them."

"They said I should look them up if I ever came to Salt Lake. Since then, they've sent me several recordings. I would like to see them again and thank them. I have their address in my little book. I'll get it for you and be right back."

"Before you go upstairs, is there anyone else?"

"If you mean Ms. Mallory, the beautiful woman from the magazine, I didn't mention her because I knew she was the first person on your list."

Andre shook his head in amazement. He had no secrets from Gerda.

"I happen to know you've been in love with her for a long time. You don't know how happy I am to see that you're finally going to do something about it." Her eyes twinkled. "The whole family has asked to meet her and thank her for honoring us as she did.

"While you're at it, why don't you invite the owner of the magazine too. Do you think he would come? I also want to thank him for sending Ms. Mallory to do the story."

"An inspirational suggestion," Andre murmured. Mr. Kinsale was an affable individual. Francesca could hardly turn down the invitation if her boss received one as well. "I'm sure he'd be delighted."

Gerda smiled before walking over to him. She put her hands on either side of his face. With tears in her blue eyes she said, "It was our lucky day when you agreed to room with us. You have always been too good to me and my family. We can't do enough for you.''

He cleared his throat. ''You already did that the night you befriended me in Zurich, and offered me a place to live. You gave me something intangible—a sense of family which I had lost.''

''I was grieving for my beloved Gunther when our family met you. You filled a hole in our hearts as well. For that I will always be grateful.''

Andre eyed her solemnly. ''So now that I finally have a way to repay you, we're even, *ja?*''

She let out a heartfelt sigh. ''*Ja, Mein Schatz.*''

As soon as she left the study, he looked up the address of the magazine.

For the last five weeks he'd worked around the clock finding a place to live, getting it furnished in time for Gerda's family. He'd even managed to spend a memorable Thanksgiving Day with Jimmy and his family.

In all that time he'd tried every technique imaginable to keep thoughts of Francesca at bay. But as he typed her name and address into the computer, it was like opening Pandora's box. Immediately he was flooded by memories of her stricken face when he told her to get out of the car. Her wounded cry still resounded in his heart.

Those signs, plus the panic she'd exhibited because they might never see each other again were the small crumbs he'd been hanging on to like a lifeline.

When he looked down, he realized his hands were trembling.

So much for his attempts to suppress all feeling!

Lord.

"Frannie? Are you there?"

"Yes, Barney."

"Drop what you're doing and come in my office, will you?"

If he wanted her right now, it had to be something important.

She dismissed the idea that this had anything to do with Andre. After five weeks of agonizing introspection, she'd told herself over and over again it was best that he'd gone out of her life for good.

Maybe her work had been slipping, and Barney was going to tell her that if she didn't snap out of her depression soon, he would have to let her go.

"I'll be right there."

"What's the matter?" Paul demanded as she got up from her desk. "You look even worse than you usually do." He was always teasing these days in an effort to cheer her.

"Thanks, Paul. Happy holidays to you too."

"Frannie, honey? You need to lighten up or you're going to crack."

"Am I that bad?"

"Only to me. If you want to talk about it, I'm available."

"I know." She took a deep breath. "Thanks for caring so much."

As soon as she entered Barney's office, he told her to sit down. "I have a surprise for both of us."

It was the last thing she had expected him to say. Intrigued, she asked what it was.

"Well, I know what mine is. Why don't you open yours and then we'll compare notes."

He handed her a letter that had come in the mail. It was addressed to Ms. Francesca

Mallory in care of the magazine. Curious, she opened it as fast as she could and pulled out a computer-generated party invitation. Her eyes scanned the contents....

Ms. Francesca Mallory and Guest are
cordially invited to attend a
Christmas Buffet on Saturday night from
seven until nine given by Gerda Richter.

"*Gerda Richter?*"

Any reminder of Andre made her pulse race. "But I thought she lived in Zurich!"

"Obviously she's staying with friends or family in Salt Lake for the holidays. That's a Federal Heights address."

"One of my favorite areas of the city," she mused. "Those beautiful older homes are classic."

"The trick these days is to be able to afford one of them." He winked.

"You're right about that."

"Why don't we make it a foursome."

"A foursome—"

"Come on now, Frannie. Don't play coy with me. Your invitation says you're supposed to bring a guest. Not that I wouldn't enjoy escorting my wife and my favorite female writer, mind you. But don't you think it's time you stopped mourning for that man, and got back in the mainstream again?''

Her face felt hot. ''I'm not in mourning.''

''You could have fooled me. I may not be a doctor, but I'd say you have one of the worst cases of lovesickitis I've seen in a long time.''

''It will pass,'' she persisted, her voice throbbing. *It has to.*

''Not without help. Isn't there another man in the cosmos you would enjoy spending a few hours with? The only way to get over a love affair gone awry is to kindle a new one. Otherwise Mr. Benet's image will remain to torture you like a hairy shirt.''

In spite of her pain, she couldn't help but laugh at the awful simile.

He laughed with her. ''That's the reaction I like to see. Now you know why I run this magazine and let you do the writing.''

She tapped the invitation against her cheek. It was time to take Barney's advice. The pain had to stop or she didn't know how she could go on living like this. If she didn't make a concerted effort to get over him, Andre would always haunt her.

At least when she phoned Howard, she could assure him that this time she really meant it.

"I tell you what. There is a man, and I think he would go with me if some woman isn't having her baby at the same time."

"Wonderful. Plan on meeting Reba and me there. We'll work out the details later on next week."

"That sounds good. You know, Barney, it was very thoughtful of Gerda to have invited you as well. But I can't say I'm surprised. Even in my short meeting with her, she came across as a kind, generous person."

"I'm looking forward to shaking her hand. That particular publication has had the highest sales figures to date this year, thanks to your expertise and her face of course."

The compliment thrilled Fran.

Maybe this could be a whole new turning point for her. She had no idea what was in store where Howard was concerned, but it would be a start in the right direction. No more looking back. Ever.

* * *

Andre finished lighting the last white candle on the wooden crèche pyramid, then surveyed the living room and foyer of his new home with a deep sense of satisfaction.

Apparently during his travels around the world, he had developed a love for the kind of large, half-timbered houses he saw while driving from Wurzburg to Fussen, an area known as ''picturebook'' Germany.

When Andre had done some serious house-hunting with his Realtor, Natalie Cairns—a striking brunette divorcee with two children—he hadn't realized how exacting his tastes would be.

Two days of searching had produced nothing. On the third day he began to lose hope of finding what he wanted. He assumed he would have to buy some property and hire an architect. That is until they reached the Federal Heights area with its woods-like feel.

When she stopped the car in front of an estate which seemed to replicate its German counterpart down to the narrow pitched roof, dark half-timbers and authentic Hapsburg yellow decor complete with window boxes, he knew he'd found the house he wanted to turn into a home.

The inside proved to be equally enchanting with its high ceilings, dark beams, fireplaces and walnut paneled study which would house the hundreds of books he'd collected over the years. In fact, he'd made many purchases which he'd put in storage, never dreaming that one day he might actually have a place to use them.

Six bedrooms, five bathrooms. There would be plenty of room for Gerda's children and grandchildren. They could occupy the upstairs while he took residence in the master bedroom and bath on the main floor.

To his delight he learned that the surrounding houses made up an exclusive, well-established neighborhood. Since he enjoyed the arts, Natalie pointed out that it was close to the university as well as the opera house and symphony hall in downtown Salt Lake.

It had all seemed right. He'd given her earnest money on the spot.

Tonight, as he took in the white lights of the seventeen-foot fir tree and heard the Christmas carols playing over the stereo, he realized he had created a place of refuge which would bring him years of pleasure.

The picture of his father—a gift from Francesca—along with a picture of his mother in a matching wood-carved frame, had been given a place of honor over the seventeenth century French escritoire, his Aunt Maudelle's prized possession. He'd placed several pictures of the two of them throughout the room to honor her memory as well.

While Gerda and her family were elsewhere taking care of last-minute details, he built up the fire in the hearth, needing something to channel his energy. The guests would start arriving within the next few minutes. If everything went according to plan, Francesca would be one of them.

Since morning he'd tried to quell the frantic hammering of his heart, but the separation from her had been of too long a duration. He no longer had any control over his emotions.

"Our first guest!" Gerda cried out from the dining room as the doorbell rang. "I'll get it!"

Andre stayed put. He had an idea it was Natalie. She'd been dropping by the house so often, it seemed that during the last week it had been on a daily basis.

From the beginning she'd made it clear that she would like to be more than broker and client. Though he knew the relationship could never go anywhere, he didn't actively discourage her because he needed her help for so many reasons, and she was an interesting person to talk to.

But when she hurried into the living room dressed in a stunning red cocktail dress and greeted him with a lingering kiss on the cheek, he saw a hunger in her eyes that made him realize he would have to put a stop to this before she got hurt.

"This house is fabulous, Andre. I mean really fabulous. The furnishings are breathtaking. I don't imagine anyone in Salt Lake has a finer collection of old world antiques than you do. I mean look at that gorgeous Russian stove or whatever you call them, not to mention the piano and tapestries."

"I'm glad you approve."

"Approve—" She whirled around to face him. "Is there something wrong with you tonight? You seem so preoccupied."

''That's probably because I am. But thanks to you and all your help, I'm convinced the party will be a huge success.''

When the doorbell sounded, his heart skipped a beat. ''Please help yourself to some hors d'oeuvres, Natalie. At this point I think I'd better start playing host.''

Within a half hour the house filled with friends, neighbors and business associates. While everyone wandered around raving about the furnishings and eating Gerda's divine food, Andre contributed to a dozen conversations both in English and German. Yet all the while he kept listening for the bell.

Each time he opened the front door, he expected to see Francesca's lovely face. But as the evening wore on and it got to be eight-fifteen, he decided neither she or the owner of the magazine were coming. Andre's disappointment was so acute, he felt as if someone had just kicked him in the gut.

Maybe the invitations had gone astray, or possibly they were still lying unopened on some secretary's desk at the office. Otherwise Francesca or her boss would surely have sent their regrets if they couldn't come.

"Andre?" Natalie joined him in the living room and tucked her arm through his. "You're so quiet I'm convinced you're not feeling well. After everyone goes home, I'll stay and help clean up."

Before he had a chance to tell her he'd hired a catering service to do that kind of work, the doorbell sounded again. His head jerked around in time to see Harbin open the front door. Suddenly four more people had stepped into the front hallway.

As Andre's gaze fell on Francesca, his breath froze in his lungs.

She'd left her gossamer hair down tonight. It floated like a cloud around her shoulders. In a long-sleeved creation of lustrous pale green velvet which modestly outlined her curves and the thrust of womanly hips, she shimmered like the spun-glass angel sitting on the credenza.

He started moving toward her. Gerda reached her first. They shook hands, then Gerda gave her a welcoming hug. At that precise moment Francesca's eyes unwittingly met Andre's. He was close enough to hear the gasp that escaped her throat.

"Andre?" she said in a breathless whisper, the green of her eyes darkening in shock.

By now she had separated herself from Gerda. Andre thought she looked like she was going to faint. Since he knew exactly how she felt, nothing could have pleased him more.

"Good evening, Francesca."

"Y-you came for Gerda's party?"

Gerda started to laugh. "Oh, no, my dear. You don't understand. This is Andre's new home. My family and I are his guests until we can buy one of our own. Like Andre, we too have decided to make our home in Salt Lake. He was kind enough to let me invite you to his housewarming party. I have to tell you he is like another son to me. I call him *mein Schatz*. My treasure.

"Now, why don't you introduce me to this handsome blond man of yours who is being so patient with us. I don't remember seeing him with you in Los Angeles."

The room reeled for Fran as Andre's parting words in the monastery parking lot rang loudly in her ears.

"If we should happen to meet again, just consider it another astounding coincidence."

Probably the hardest thing Fran had ever had to do in her life was smile and make introductions while her world had just been turned upside down. Gerda seemed anxious to talk to Barney. Eventually she ushered him and his wife into the dining room, but Fran couldn't move.

She stood there in shock trying to absorb the earthshaking revelation that for the last five weeks, while she'd been grieving because he'd probably left America, Andre hadn't gone anywhere. Instead, he had bought a home in one of the nicest areas of Salt Lake and was living in it. Yet he hadn't once tried to contact her.

But why would he? a little voice nagged.

It was she who had gone to Andre the last time to end things once and for all. She'd even told him there was another man in her life; therefore she had absolutely no right to be hurt by this knowledge. No right at all.

But she *was* hurt. In fact she was devastated....

As for Gerda Richter, Fran couldn't fathom that she and her family had moved here either, or that her son had been appointed associate professor of German at the university. If it hadn't been for Gerda wanting to meet her again, Fran wouldn't be a guest in Andre's home right now.

Maybe she was dreaming.

But the tall, dark, powerful-looking man wearing an expensive navy silk suit with a white shirt and elegant striped tie was no figment of her imagination. His hair had grown a little longer. An urbane sophistication clung to him.

It was impossible to take her eyes off him, but she had to for decency's sake. For Howard's sake! Good heavens. She'd forgotten about him.

If her heart didn't stop pounding so hard, she was afraid it might do real damage. She pressed her hand over it as if she could slow it down, but the gesture proved futile.

"Howard?" she struggled to make conversation. "Andre Benet is the son of Abbot Ambrose, the man I wrote about in my article for the magazine. He was the one who gave me the interview in his father's place.

"Mr. Benet, this is Dr. Howard Barker."

"I read the piece with great interest and can see the resemblance," Howard murmured in a mild-mannered voice. "Your father was a remarkable man. I'm sorry to hear that he passed away."

"Thank you, Dr. Barker. I just wish I'd had a little more time with him, but it wasn't meant to be. Are your parents still living?"

"Yes."

"You're very fortunate."

"Howard's father is a wonderful man too," Fran felt obligated to say something, though she wished the floor would simply open up and devour her. "He's the pastor of my church," she added quietly.

"Is that so?" Andre replied, eyeing Howard speculatively. "It seems you and I have quite a bit in common then, being the sons of men who've devoted their lives to God. Unlike our parents, both of us managed to go in another direction."

Howard's mouth twitched. "You're right. In fact I find myself having to apologize for my choice of profession at least once a day."

Andre's dark, penetrating gaze unexpectedly swerved to Fran. "That's where the good doctor and I differ. When you've been a rolling stone for as long as I have, no one knows enough about you to make a comment like that.''

While Fran tried to remain unaffected by his pointed remark Howard asked, ''What is it you do for a living?''

Fran couldn't believe both men were carrying on this conversation as if they were enjoying it.

''Apart from the time I attended university in Switzerland, I spent most of my life at sea. Now I deal in investments of various kinds.''

What university?

What kind of investments?

''Andre?'' an unfamiliar female voice jerked Fran from her stupor. She turned her head in time to watch a beautiful brunette woman in a revealing red dress approach him. She took hold of his arm with such confidence, it told its own story. Fran felt as if she'd just been stabbed repeatedly in the heart. ''I don't believe I've met your guests.''

Suavely he said, ''This is Natalie Cairns, my Realtor. Without her help I would never have known this home was privately listed, let alone that I would be able to move in this fast. Natalie, may I present Francesca Mallory, a writer for *Beehive Magazine,* and her friend, Dr. Howard Barker, the newest obstetrician in town.''

''Really?'' Her brown eyes sparkled up at Howard. ''Do you need help finding a place to live?''

''Actually I do.''

Fran blinked. She could scarcely credit any of this was happening, let alone that Howard would leave himself open like that.

''I've been staying with my parents while I've had to see about my practice, but now I'm anxious to find a place of my own, probably a condo. Naturally I'd prefer a home like Mr. Benet's here. This is an extraordinary house. But I'm a poor, struggling doctor right now, so I won't be able to set my sights as high.''

Natalie broke into a full-bodied smile. ''Another year or two and I'll be happy to find you something equally beautiful. In the meantime, let me give you my card before you leave the party, and we'll get together this week. My purse is upstairs. If you'll excuse me for a minute, Dr. Barker. I'll be right back.'' She whispered something against Andre's cheek before dashing off.

Her familiarity with him was almost more than Fran could bear. She needed to be alone to get some composure back.

''Howard? While you're waiting for her, why don't I go in the dining room and fix us a couple of plates.''

''Good idea. I'll join you in a minute.''

Without looking at either man, she hurried through the tall French doors off the foyer leading to the dining room. It had an old-world, medieval charm with its high ceiling and arched beams. A tapestry hung over one wall.

She sucked in her breath at the beauty of the standing candelabras and tapers, the magnificent table with its centerpiece of flowers and greenery. A Christmas tree stood in one corner, covered with tiny red lights and adorable hand-painted, wooden ornaments.

With such fabulous furnishings and food, it was no wonder everyone lingered to talk and eat. Andre had provided a veritable feast. She'd come to the party with an appetite, but it had deserted her the second she'd seen him.

‘‘Gerda made all these dishes. Try her apple and cinnamon strudel. It’s an old family recipe to die for,’’ Andre murmured near her ear.

At the sound of his low voice, Fran almost dropped the plate she was preparing for Howard. Without conscious thought she lifted her gaze to his.

‘‘What’s going on, Andre?’’ she cried in a tremulous voice. ‘‘The last time we were together, you led me to believe I would never see you again. I presumed you had gone back to sea.’’ She bit her lip in an effort to tamp down her emotions. ‘‘N-Now I find you here, ensconced in this beautiful home with Gerda and her family as your houseguests.’’

‘‘Do you like the things I’ve acquired over the years?’’ he asked in a smooth tone. ‘‘I thought why not uncrate my treasures and find a permanent place for them. They go well in this house, don’t you think?’’

Fran had trouble catching her breath. ‘‘You don’t need me to answer that question,’’ she said, her voice trembling. ‘‘Please, Andre,’’ she begged. ‘‘Tell me the truth. Why have you done all this?’’

He studied her through shuttered eyes so she couldn't read their expression. "You know damn well why." His voice carried the sting of a whiplash. "You're the only reason I've settled in Salt Lake."

Her eyes widened at his bald honesty. "But—"

"But—" he interrupted before she could say anything else "—I didn't tell you everything on my mind the last time we were together because, if you recall, you intimated you had come to the monastery to end things with me on a civil note. You also said there was an important man in your life. Dr. Barker is that man, isn't he?"

Like lightning, he'd changed the subject. Her heart raced faster. She would be a liar if she said no. "I've known Howard since I was a little girl."

"You two look good together. He has the right family, all the right credentials. I can see in his eyes he's crazy about you."

Stop, Andre.

"When you've been at sea with as many different kinds of men as I have over the years, you learn to read them very well. I like Dr.

Barker. I think you've met your match, Francesca. If I were a betting man, I would wager he'll be faithful to you to the end of your days.''

She was shaking so hard, she had to put the plate down.

''Does he know I'm the man he was worried about?''

''After tonight, I'm sure he does.''

''How so?''

''You know why,'' she whispered heatedly. ''Until I saw you standing behind Gerda, I had no idea this was your house, or that Barney and I had been invited to your party. Howard couldn't have helped but notice my shock.''

''He handled it admirably.''

''Please, can we stop talking about him.''

''Of course,'' he said with enviable quiescence. ''What would you like to talk about?''

She averted her eyes. ''W-We don't need to talk about anything. You have dozens of guests whom you're neglecting.''

''I'd rather talk to you. If the truth be known, I'd rather do a great deal more to you than talk. It's been a long time, Francesca,'' he said, his voice grating.

Dear God.

"How can you say that to me?" she muttered furiously because he'd touched upon the one subject that kept her awake nights.

"I may be many things, but I'm not a man to lie about my feelings. I wanted you from the moment you walked in the monastery gift shop. I still want you." By now her whole body was trembling. "In my gut I know you want me too," he said huskily.

"So does Natalie Cairns," she fired at him because she was in so much pain.

"I needed a real estate agent. She was invited to this party as my way of repaying her for her hard work. After tonight, I won't be seeing her again. You're the only woman I'm interested in."

"For how long?" she cried, hugging her arms to her waist.

A palpable tension leaped between them. "I could ask you the same question. Do you honestly think women have the monopoly on that fear? Do you have any idea how many married sailors who've been true to their wives have hurried home to them after a long stint at sea only to find them in their own bed with another man?''

His question was one she'd never given any real thought to before. Her head reared back so she could look at him. ''You think I could be capable of doing that?''

A grimace marred his attractive features. ''I have no idea,'' he said in all solemnity.

They stared long and hard at each other until she admitted, ''I-I realize there are no guarantees.''

''A man and a woman who are strong enough, come together willing to take the risk. My parents slept with each other one last time knowing full well they would never see each other again.

''My father's heart was torn because he loved her, yet he felt called to the priesthood. My mother knew this and unselfishly kept the knowledge of her pregnancy to herself. Because they risked, she died giving birth to me.''

''Oh, Andre—'' she cried softly, her heart melting for the little boy inside him who'd grieved for the parents he'd been denied. ''I don't know how you've been able to bear your father's death as well as you have."

"It's because we made our peace with each other before he died. Would that you and your father will be able to do the same one day, no matter what he did to you."

She shook her head. "I don't want to see him."

"I felt the same way when Aunt Maudelle confessed on her deathbed that my father was still alive somewhere in the world. It means putting your feelings at risk once more."

"You're obviously stronger than I am."

"Don't be deceived," he warned in a grave voice. "I've been living for the moment when you walked through my front door. If you touched me right now, you would feel me trembling. That's how much I desire you."

Heat flooded her face. Her emotions were so traumatized, it was impossible to articulate with any coherence. "Andre— I thin—"

"Fran?"

At the sound of her name being called out with some urgency, she jerked around with a guilty start. Howard walked swiftly toward her. "While I was discussing condos with

Natalie, I got a call on my beeper and have to leave for the hospital. My patient's about ready to deliver. Barney will run you home.''

Afraid of being left alone with Andre she said, ''I'm coming with you.''

He shook his head. ''I have no idea how long I'll be. I'd rather you stayed here and enjoyed the party.''

Though he would never have let on, she could tell Howard was upset. He extended his hand to Andre. ''Thank you for your hospitality. Sorry I have to rush out.''

''I understand. Thank you for coming,'' came the bland reply.

''Fran?'' Howard gave her an enigmatic glance. ''I'll call you tomorrow.''

She would have asked him to phone her later tonight, but with Andre standing there hearing every word, the tension was so palpable she had a feeling Howard would rebuff that suggestion as well.

''I'll be waiting. I hope everything goes well.''

He nodded to both of them before walking off.

As soon as he'd left the dining room she heard Andre say, "Being an obstetrician's wife will have its challenges, but then every worthwhile relationship requires sacrifice."

Fran's jaw hardened. "If you'll excuse me—"

"Where do you think you're going so fast?" In the next instant, he had caught hold of her wrist.

"Please let go of me," she cried in panic because his touch had ignited her senses. "People will notice."

"They won't if you don't make a scene. Now tell me why you're so angry."

"Because you planned all this!"

"You can lay a lot of blame at my feet, but I don't have the kind of power to send a woman into labor on cue."

"You know what I mean."

"If you're referring to this party, then you're right. I gave it to help Gerda and her family feel more at home. They're people in a strange country who want to belong. I know the feeling well."

There he went again, trying to arouse her compassion.

"But if I'd known it was your house, I would never have come," she said through clenched teeth.

"You knew Gerda was a dear friend of mine," he inserted sinuously. "Can you honestly stand there and tell me you didn't hope I might be here too?"

Her breath caught. "If I did, then it was subconscious," she admitted with reluctance. "Otherwise I would never have invited Howard to come with me. He's the last person in the world I would want to hurt."

"If there were nothing between you and me, he couldn't be hurt. But as we all learned tonight, the truth can no longer be ignored." He seemed to be holding his emotions barely in check. "I'm taking you home later."

Her legs started to shake. "No, Andre. I'm leaving with Barney."

"You do that and I'll follow you in my car."

"You can't abandon your guests!" she cried out aghast.

"Watch me."

"Andre— Please—"

''Say that to me when we're alone, and I'll put us both out of our misery. Now I suggest you go in the other room and let your boss know you have another way home. Or shall I do it for you?''

All the while he was talking, he smoothed his thumb over her palm before letting her hand go. She didn't know if it was deliberate or not, but it sent a message her body couldn't ignore.

With her heart tripping over itself, she practically ran from the dining room in her haste to put distance between them.

By the time she found Barney standing in Andre's living room talking to a group of people, she was out of breath.

As soon as her boss saw her, he started toward her and chuckled. ''I wish you could have seen the look on your face a little while ago. It would make a great front cover.''

Barney saw too much.

She cleared her throat. ''Where's Reba?''

''In the ladies' room. She spilled punch on her dress and wanted to get the worst of it out before it dried. Since we're alone for the moment, why don't you tell me why you allowed that lovely thing in red to corner Howard before he left for the hospital.''

''I didn't allow anything!'' she retorted defensively. ''After he learned she was a Realtor, *he* was the one who wanted to discuss business with her.''

Barney appeared to ponder her response before he said, ''As soon as Reba comes back, we'll leave together and I'll drive you home.''

''Actually, I've already been offered a ride, but thank you anyway,'' she said in a small voice. There was no use lying to Barney. He knew everything anyway.

After a pause, ''Mr. Benet's methods are unorthodox to say the least, but they produce results. He has accomplished what I didn't expect to see happen in my lifetime.''

''What are you talking about?'' she snapped.

''Why don't you tell *me* at the office on Monday morning, if you dare. Good-night, Frannie.''

He gave her a peck on the cheek before leaving her alone to contemplate the rest of the night ahead of her with fear and apprehension.

CHAPTER SEVEN

IN A KIND OF DAZE, Fran found herself staring at a photograph placed next to the one she'd given Andre of his distinguished father.

The young, dark-haired woman in the picture had long black hair and dark-fringed black eyes, identical to Andre's.

His mother was breathtaking. *Just like her son.*

Seeing her likeness helped Fran to imagine how hard it must have been for Andre's father to give her up. But give her up, he did, thus denying both mother and son the joy of family.

How sad that she had died without being able to raise her perfect little boy and watch him grow into such an incredibly attractive man.

Drawn to everything about Andre, she moved to the other end of the room to look at a grouping of small photographs on an Italian provincial credenza.

Andre, her heart cried out as she recognized the promise of the man in his boyish features. He'd probably been nine or ten when the picture was taken. In shorts and a shirt, he stood hand in hand with an older woman who was probably his aunt. He appeared tall for his age.

She picked up the other two photographs both taken at the same time. Neither he or his aunt smiled in any of them. Fran ached for the pain he and his entire family had been forced to endure.

Afraid the tears would start, she put the pictures back and hurried from the living room, anxious to find a place to be alone. As the far end of the hall she glimpsed a library through the French doors which were ajar.

Consumed by her need to know everything about Andre, she peeked inside. To her relief, no one else was there. With relief, she closed the doors and went over to the closest bookshelf which stretched from floor to ceiling.

Among other things, Andre appeared to be a history buff. She pulled out a tome on the Romans. *From the Gracchi to Nero.*

Unlike some *nouveau riche* who created a room in a home like this for show, he'd spent many years at sea and had probably read every book in sight. His choice of reading material was one of the differences she could see about him from his father.

While Fran had been doing some research on Abbot Ambrose in the archives at Catholic church headquarters, she'd discovered that he'd been a scholar who, in addition to having written many treatises of his own for publication, had built up an enviable library of religious texts for the monastery.

Losing track of time, she thumbed through the book in her hand, then reached for another, fascinated by this treasure-trove of information.

Without having sensed that anyone was in the library with her, she suddenly felt masculine hands slide on to her shoulders and knead them with gentle pressure.

''Andre—'' she cried out softly. In the next instant, the book she'd been holding slipped to the parquet floor.

''I'm glad you found a subject to interest you,'' he whispered as his lips kissed the side of her neck. ''But now that we're finally alone, I can think of something infinitely more satisfying for both of us. *Lord*—to finally have you in my arms like this—''

His hands moved down her arms to her hips, then slid around to her stomach, molding her to his strong, hard body. This time there was no car door separating them.

Moaning her need, she turned helplessly in his arms and lifted her mouth to find the scorching ecstasy of his. The second it closed over hers she was once again lost in an explosion of desire that rocked her to the very foundations.

Without conscious thought she wrapped her arms around his neck, desperate to get as close to him as their clothes and bodies would allow.

''I want you, Francesca,'' he murmured huskily, kissing her eyes, her nose, her ears, her neck and mouth over and over again, until they were moving and breathing as living extensions of each other.

''These months of seeing you for only a few minutes at a time, unable to do anything about the ache growing inside of me, have driven me out of my mind. I want you more than anything I've ever wanted in my life.''

Fran had no defense against that kind of admission because she felt the same way. Something told her he wasn't lying. ''I-I want you too, Andre,'' her voice trembled, ''But—''

His deep groan of satisfaction ignored her protest. Caressing her arms he whispered, ''Stay the night with me, darling. The guests and the help have left the house. Gerda and her family have gone upstairs to bed.''

The temptation to do whatever he wanted took her to the very edge of sanity. But at the last second she cried, ''Much as I want to sleep with you, Andre, I-I couldn't!''

''Why?'' he demanded, staring down at her out of dark eyes glazed with passion while his hands still held her in place. ''I realize you're an innocent. I would never do anything you didn't want me to do. Don't you know I would never hurt you?''

Fran knew that. ''You don't understand. That's not the reason, Andre.''

''Then it's because you're afraid I'll be gone again when you wake up in the morning.''

''No!'' She averted her eyes, trying unsuccessfully to hide the truth from his probing gaze.

"You're lying, Francesca, but I have a solution, one I've been thinking about for some time. We'll drive to Nevada and get married tonight."

Fran gasped as her heart turned over. She lifted her head and gazed up helplessly at him. "*Married—*"

He kissed her astounded mouth with a hunger to match the clamoring needs of her body. "I would have proposed first. But knowing of your distrust of men, I thought you would tell me that the only way you would come willingly to my bed was to have a short-term affair with no promises or expectations."

She quivered in his arms because he understood her far too well for her own good.

"Don't you know an affair is the last thing I want?" he asked, his voice grating. "Why else do you think I bought this home if not to live in it with my bride? I've never asked any woman to marry me, but I'm asking you." The rasp in his voice resonated to her insides.

She clung to him in shock. If she'd heard him correctly, he'd just asked her to be his wife.

With his lips buried in her silky hair he said, "I suggested getting married in Nevada for several reasons. In the first place, I need you tonight, darling. It's going to be difficult, if not impossible to stop kissing you once I start. Marriage will allow us the freedom to love each other the way we've been yearning to do since last April.

"Secondly, I know you care about Dr. Barker and wouldn't want to hurt him by asking his father to marry us in front of your whole family and congregation.

"Since we can't be married in your church without causing other people pain, then a private ceremony in Nevada, which is in easy driving distance, is as good a place as any to begin our life together.

"We *are* meant to be together, Francesca," he said in low tones. "You know that as well as I do. You also know that every separation has torn us apart a little more. Tonight we can end the torment and get in each other's arms where we want and need to be on a permanent basis," he continued, his voice shaking.

"While you think over my proposal, I'm going to turn out the lights and lock up the house.

When I come back in this room, I want an answer.''

''Andre—'' she blurted in pain and tore herself free of his embrace. With her chest heaving she said, ''You can't say all these earth-shaking things to me and then expect me to give you an answer in a matter of minutes!''

''I already have,'' came his clipped response with that note of finality. ''You and I have had months apart to ponder our situation. Tonight we've reached the point where there's no going back.'' His handsome face had darkened with lines. ''Either we're together, or we're not. It's entirely up to you.''

In a few swift strides he disappeared from the library, leaving her a mass of nerves.

She knew with every fiber of her being he meant what he said.

This party tonight had been his way of letting her know he was perfectly serious about wanting a solid relationship with her. He'd gone so far as to actually buy a home, which meant he'd given up his life at sea to propose marriage to her.

It was true they'd spent little time together, but because of the unique circumstances of their meeting, she knew the important things about his life and background. She'd met his friend Gerda and her family who patently adored him.

If she were honest with herself, she would have to admit that spending any more private time with him without being able to express her physical love would be next to impossible.

Something about Andre brought her to a feverish pitch just thinking about him. All he had to do was caress her hand, or brush his fingers against her hip and she dissolved in his arms.

How could anyone hold out against the onslaught of such powerful needs?

Fran knew she couldn't. She was hopelessly in love with him. For months she'd wanted, dreamed of loving him without any attendant guilt.

The idea of marriage to him tonight would satisfy those needs and legitimize what they felt for each other.

Andre had been right about a lot of things. By driving to Nevada, they would avoid placing the Barkers in an untenable position, not to mention Fran's mother who'd secretly hoped Fran would marry Howard.

But she knew there was a downside to all this. If she told him she couldn't marry him, he would go away. Her heart whispered that this time, *it was all or nothing.*

She'd already lived through the shattering, devastating experience of saying goodbye to him too many times in the past. It was doubtful she could live through it again without traumatic consequences.

There was no use lying to herself anymore. Ever since she'd received Gerda's invitation, she'd secretly prayed Andre would be at the Christmas party, that he hadn't gone out of her life for good.

Tonight, to her joy, she'd been given one last reprieve to consider what it would be like to never see him again, to never be kissed by him again or held in his arms.

Since she couldn't contemplate a life without him—since she refused to have an affair—marriage appeared to be the only answer.

In the deepest recesses of her being Fran realized she was irrevocably in love with him. Her heart had known it from the moment they'd clashed in the monastery gift shop on that first day when she'd found herself fatally attracted to him.

Of course she had no idea how long their marriage would last. She didn't expect it to last. Since her constancy wasn't in question here, she would have to wait until Andre decided he'd had enough and wanted out. That was the price she would have to pay for loving him.

But when she considered the alternative of watching him walk out of her life tonight, never to come back again, there was no contest.

Before she lost her nerve, she needed to find him. She left the library on a run. ''Oh—'' she cried out in surprise when she collided with a hard male chest outside the French doors.

Andre's strong arms closed around her, bringing her to a standstill. When she gazed up at him, his striking features looked etched in stone. His body felt rock-hard.

''Are you so frightened of your own feelings, you can't even face me, and must resort to sneaking out of my house like a thief in the night?''

She shook her head. ''No, Andre. I wasn't running away. You've misunderstood. I was coming to find you and tell you that—that I'll marry you.''

Her declaration resonated in the hallway.

In the next instance she heard him struggle to catch his breath. ''You mean that?'' he asked in a low, vibrant voice.

Fran swallowed hard. ''Yes. I mean it,'' she admitted quietly, realizing there was no going back now.

In the semidark hall, she couldn't read the expression in his eyes, but she sensed some of the tension go out of him. His hands kneaded her shoulders with growing insistence, sending fingers of delight through her body. ''That's all I needed to hear.''

Before she could tell him she loved him, his possessive mouth descended and once again they were devouring each other. But this time there was a difference.

This time she didn't have to suppress her feelings or worry that she would never see him again. It was heaven to be able to give in to the burning tide of desire which threatened to consume her, and left her clinging to him.

"Elko is three hours from here," he said in a thick-toned voice, sounding as shaken by their passion as she was. "We can be married and stay the night," he murmured against her lips as if he could never get enough of them.

"I have to be home by tomorrow morning. Howard will be phoning me at my apartment and—"

"I'm perfectly aware you have unfinished business where he's concerned," Andre interrupted, then gave her another soul-destroying kiss. "We'll be back in time, but right now all I can think about is making you my wife. Under the circumstances, three hours sounds like three years and I don't plan to waste another second. Let's go."

In a euphoric stupor, Fran walked through the house with him, aware of his hand at the back of her neck, gently guiding her while he caressed the hot skin with his fingers.

Experiencing a sense of déjà vu, she climbed in his elegant Mercedes. Once they were both settled, he backed the car out of the garage and they were off. It occurred to her that except for her purse, she didn't even have a bag packed. No toothbrush, no change of clothes. Nothing.

"Andre—" she started to speak, but he cut her off.

"Don't spoil it, Francesca. For once in your life, just go with your senses. All that either of us will require is each other."

The next thing she knew, his hand had slid to her thigh. It remained there, sending rivers of heat coursing through her body.

After they'd left the city limits he whispered, "Do you have any idea how long I've dreamed of this moment?"

"I-I think I do," she answered breathlessly.

His fingers played with the velvet material covering her flesh, driving her mad with desire.

"Before I met you, I used to watch the men when we'd arrive in port after a long haul at sea. The ones who had wives and children waiting for them would be first off the ship.

"My friend, Jimmy, couldn't wait till we were tied up to the dock. After final chores were done, he'd be the first up on deck so he could spot her red hair. When he found her, he would shout to her and his family, his eyes glowing like hot coals, his whole wiry body trembling with excitement and anticipation.

"I couldn't imagine what it would be like to feel that way about a woman, to live for the moment when I could finally be reunited with my wife and children, wanting for nothing else.

"Whatever that elusive element was, it had always escaped me. That is—" He paused and turned his head, sending her an all-encompassing gaze. "Until the morning I knew you were coming back to the monastery with the rough draft of your article.

"Long before you walked through the gift shop door, I found myself waiting for you, imagining you bringing the sunshine inside with you, imagining the scent of your skin, visualizing the way your beautiful body would look in some feminine outfit as you walked toward me."

With every private revelation, Fran thrilled and trembled a little more.

"When I heard footsteps, my heart began skittering all over the place like the sparks of a ship's magneto. That's when I knew something earthshaking had happened to me.

"At first I fought my feelings because they were too overpowering."

"I know, because I felt exactly the same way when I drove to the monastery that morning," she confessed quietly. "It's embarrassing how much I wanted to see you again. But overriding those feelings was this terrible shadow of guilt. I couldn't believe I was enamored of a man who'd taken a vow of celibacy." She shivered in remembrance. "I'm afraid I didn't fight my feelings nearly as hard as I should have."

"Thank God."

He squeezed her leg gently, then tousled her hair. "You sounded sleepy just now. Why don't you close your eyes and get some rest while you can."

His comment was a reminder of the wedding night to come. Suffused in heat, she did his bidding. At first her heart was pounding so hard, she didn't think it was possible to lose consciousness. But at some point, her body must have succumbed to all the emotion draining her. She didn't waken until she heard Andre's seductive voice calling to her.

"We've arrived, Francesca." He kissed her so thoroughly, she was witless after he let her go. "It's time."

"I can't believe we're here. You shouldn't have let me sleep so long. I could have spelled you off driving."

"I enjoyed it, and you obviously needed the rest. Here's your purse," he said as she began groping for it. Andre seemed to have the ability to read her mind.

Her hands shook slightly as she ran a brush through her hair and reapplied the lipstick he'd kissed off back at the house. Once she felt presentable, she got out of the car on shaky legs, thankful for his support.

As they entered the small white chapel, a newly-married couple passed them on their way out the door. Neither of them looked a day over eighteen, and certainly not old enough to get married.

Andre ushered Fran toward the front of the chapel where two elderly couples waited for them.

"Good morning," said the woman behind the desk. "I'm Mrs. Appleby. This is my husband, Judge Appleby. He'll be performing the ceremony. Mr. and Mrs. Granville will stand in as witnesses. If you'll fill out the form for the wedding license, then we can begin. Do you plan to exchange rings?''

''I do,'' Andre answered to Fran's complete astonishment before he started signing papers.

''You bought a ring?'' Fran asked incredulously.

With a quiet smile Andre stood up and pulled a plain gold band out of his suit pocket. ''It's the only possession my father left me before he died. He bought it with the intention of asking my mother to marry him. But she knew his religious leanings too well and urged him to join the priesthood instead, so he kept it.''

Fran put the back of her hand to her mouth so she wouldn't cry out. That ring was precious. It represented his parents' love as well as their struggle.

''That will be a hundred dollars, please.''

Andre repocketed the ring, then reached for his wallet. Fran watched him put a five-hundred-dollar bill on top of the table. ''Keep the change, Mrs. Appleby. Consider it a gift from Francesca and myself because you're willing to accommodate us at this unorthodox hour.''

''That's very generous of you, Mr. Benet. We'll use it to help those couples who don't have enough money for the license. Now, if your fiancée will sign the bottom line, the Judge can begin the ceremony.''

Taking a deep breath, Fran picked up the pen. Earlier in the evening while she'd been getting ready to go to Gerda's party with Howard, if someone had told her she would be getting married to Andre Benet in Elko, Nevada, before the night was over, she would have scoffed at such a ludicrous notion.

Yet here she was with him, ready to enter into the most sacred ceremony between a man and a woman.

Dear God. What was she doing?

Mrs. Appleby handed her husband the papers for him to look over.

''Francesca Mallory, Andre Benet?'' the judge said their names, adjusting his bifocals. ''I was going to tell you to take each other by the hand, but I can see you've already done that. Please approach the pulpit.''

Andre's fingers tightened around hers as he drew her alongside him, then stood tall to face the judge.

"I see here that this is a first marriage for both of you."

"That's right," Andre murmured while Fran nodded, feeling more and more anxious.

"You're both old enough to know what you're doing, but nobody knows what marriage is like because that sacred institution is what I like to call 'uncharted waters.' A sailor would know what I'm talking about."

Fran's gaze darted to Andre whose compelling mouth curved in a knowing half smile. Instead of reassuring her, that smile filled her with unease.

Uncharted waters.

That was exactly what it felt like.

What did she really know about Andre? It wasn't a question of love. There was no doubt she was in love with him. Mindlessly in love.

But there was still so much she and Andre ought to know about each other before they made a commitment as binding as marriage.

"It means you've got to be prepared for anything," the Judge spoke on, ignorant of her turmoil. ''And there's only one way to do that.''

He took off his glasses and rubbed the bridge of his nose before putting them back on. Then leaning on the pulpit and looking both of them straight in the eye he said, ''All you have to do is put your partner's happiness before your own.

''That's all!'' His hands spread wide. ''That's it! That's the trick! Unselfishness gets the job done through the good weather and the bad. When the children come, they bring more joy, but more pressures.

''After you leave this chapel, if you promise in your heart and soul to put your spouse's happiness ahead of your own, *every time,* you'll not only make it through this life with all it holds in store for you, you'll find joy.''

The sleep in the car must have cleared Fran's head because the gravity of what she was about to do hit her full force.

Her love for Andre was greater than she'd thought possible. But the Judge's words stabbed her conscience. She couldn't honestly promise before God to put Andre's happiness ahead of her own every time. Not when she didn't even know what made him happy.

He'd bought a home, ostensibly for them to live in. He obviously had money, investments, which could take care of them. But she wasn't ready to live there with him yet, not when she worried he might grow tired next week or next month of a traditional lifestyle and yearn for the sea.

While they were on fire for each other, the idea of settling down held great appeal. But later on, he would probably feel confined. Then would come the anger and the reproaches because she would sense his restlessness and start to act possessive of his time.

When he left, she wouldn't be able to face people knowing she hadn't been able to hold her husband's love. She'd rather die than repeat her mother's history. It would be better to keep their marriage a secret for a while and live in separate households.

As for children, neither she or Andre had even touched on the subject.

A long time ago Fran had made the decision that if she ever did marry, she would never bring a child into the world. To give birth would be to experience another form of hell if the baby's father abandoned them both.

But after what Andre had told her in the car, it sounded like he wanted children, even craved them.

Once more an image of the magnificent house he'd bought flashed through her mind. It was a big home. Too big for two people to rattle around in.

Maybe because she and Andre had run away to be married in a place that wasn't a real church with a real pastor, she hadn't expected to be affected by the Judge's words.

But to her shock, everything he'd said ran soul deep and filled her with fresh apprehension.

"Now repeat after me. I, Francesca Mallory, take this man, Andre Benet, to be my lawfully wedded husband."

She tried to swallow, but her mouth had gone dry. "I-I," she began, but she couldn't get the words out. They wouldn't come. She tried again.

Andre's arm slipped around her waist and he pulled her close. "What's the matter, darling?'' he whispered. ''You're so pale. Are you ill?''

''Yes,'' she grasped the excuse like a lifeline. Except that it wasn't an excuse at this point. She really did feel physically sick. ''I-I can't go through with this, Andre. It has all happened too fast. Forgive me.''

She looked up at the Judge. ''Forgive me, Your Honor.''

''It's all right, Ms. Mallory.'' His smile was kind. ''Better to wait until you know you can say your vows without hesitation. You're a brave woman. I admire you for your courage.

''I'm sure your fiancé, Mr. Benet, wouldn't want you to make a solemn oath you're not ready to make, any more than you would want him to take vows if there were still things left unresolved between you.

''My advice is to go home and reason this out together. If your love is meant to be, time will show you the way.''

Tears filled her eyes as the Judge moved from behind his lectern and gave her a fatherly hug.

When he released her, she heard Andre quietly thank the Judge and his wife for their time before he cupped her elbow and escorted her from the chapel.

"Andre—" she cried his name in pain after he'd helped her into the car and they'd pulled away from the curb.

"It's all right, Francesca."

"No, it's not! But I'm frightened, Andre. I-I need more time to think."

"I understand."

Her breath caught. "After I told you I would marry you tonight, I don't see how you could understand anything! You have every right to despise me," she murmured with self-loathing.

"I wouldn't be human if I didn't admit I'm disappointed. But as for despising you, I think you already know the answer to that."

He was being far too controlled for a man who'd just been rejected at the altar. "A-Are you going to leave Salt Lake now?"

He turned his head to stare at her. "Is that what you want me to do?"

She fought to get control of her emotions, but she was fast losing the battle. "I want you to do what *you* want to do," she blurted before she buried her face in her hands and broke down sobbing.

"Then that's exactly what I'll do."

They drove to her apartment in tension-filled silence. His last comment had raised pure terror in her heart.

"You don't have to see me to the door," she said as she struggled to get out of the car.

He ignored her comment and came around to the passenger side to help her out. By the time they reached her apartment inside the building, she was a mass of nerve endings screaming for release from pain.

Andre would never want her now. Who could blame him?

She opened her purse and fumbled for the key. He ended up finding it. Soon her apartment door stood ajar.

"Andre—" She lifted a ravaged, tearstained face to him.

"Don't say anything you might have to take back," he warned.

On that quelling note he kissed her hard on the mouth before walking away.

CHAPTER EIGHT

THE DOORBELL SOUNDED AGAIN. "Fran? Are you home, honey?"

Fran could hear her mother calling to her. Disoriented, she lifted her head from the pillow and stared bleary-eyed at the clock by her bed. Ten after twelve?

Andre had dropped her off a little around four this morning. After collapsing in a paroxysm of tears, she must have finally cried herself to sleep.

"Just a minute," she shouted back. "I'm coming."

Staggering off the mattress, she threw on her velour robe and hurried through her small two-bedroom apartment to the front door.

"Mom?" She had to smooth the hair out of her eyes to see her.

"Fran, honey—" Her mother hugged her hard. "Thank heavens you answered the door. Everyone has been trying to get hold of you.

I was just about to let myself in to see if you were too sick to get out of bed.''

''I'm all right,'' she murmured guiltily.

Her mother stared at her with probing hazel eyes. ''You don't look it. What's wrong, honey? Where have you been? Howard has been trying to reach you since last night.''

What?

''His patient went into false labor and was released, so he went back to the party for you.''

Fran groaned.

''But it was all over by the time he got there, and Mr. Benet's houseguest, Mrs. Richter, had no idea where anyone was. So Howard called Barney, thinking you must be at Barney's house because he was the one who had driven you home.

''That's when he found out you had accepted Mr. Benet's offer of a ride home instead. Howard became alarmed when he started calling you at ten this morning and still couldn't reach you.''

I'm sorry, Howard. I'm so sorry.

''I kept trying to get you, and finally decided to come over myself. When I saw your car in the garage, that's when I really started to worry.''

A shuddering breath escaped Fran's lips. ''I'm sorry to have upset you. Come in and sit down, Mom.''

Fran shut the door, but her mother still stood there.

''I realize you're twenty-eight years old and can take care of yourself. What you do is your own business. But when I phoned Mrs. Richter before I drove over here just now, she told me Mr. Benet still hadn't home come yet. She was worried because in the past he has always kept her informed of his whereabouts. At that point I'm afraid we both feared the worst, that you'd been involved in a car accident or something.''

Oh, no.

Andre had gone....

The world started to reel.

''Honey?''

Her mother grabbed her arm. ''Come on. Sit down on the couch. You've gone pale as a ghost. Let me get you some water.''

''Thanks, Mom,'' she said when her mother brought her a drink from the kitchen. The cold water actually tasted good and helped restore her somewhat. She drained it before setting it down on the coffee table.

Her mother had a way of seeing right through her. Fran hadn't planned to tell her about last night in order to save her any grief. But now that her mother was here, she deserved an explanation. There was nothing to do but tell her the truth.

"Mom?" she began in a wobbly voice. "Last night after the party, Andre asked me to marry him. I-I told him yes, so we drove to Elko."

"Honey!" her mother cried out with pure joy and started to get up to hug her.

"Let me finish, Mom," Fran said when she could see her mother's excitement. She kneaded her hands together. "We were halfway through the ceremony w-when I couldn't go through with the rest of it. I have to say it was the most traumatic experience of my entire life.

"Andre brought me back early this morning. I was so horrified by what I'd done to him, I cried all the way home. Naturally I'll never see him again. What Mrs. Richter told you just verifies it.

"After I got in bed, I cried for hours. When I finally fell asleep, I didn't hear anything. I-I'm sorry you had to come over and find me like this."

All the joy had left her mother's face, making her look older. "I'm sorry too," she whispered. Fran's parent was such an upbeat person, it hurt Fran to hear the desolation in her mother's voice.

Fran shook her head in pained confusion. "Why are *you* sorry, Mom? I thought you hoped Howard and I would get together one day."

"You're wrong, honey. I let go of that dream for you by high school. To be honest, I never expected you to marry at all. But just now, when you told me you had eloped to Elko, I was so happy I wanted to shout it to the heavens.

"I thought, at last my daughter has met a man who has managed to get past those barriers she erected years ago. But obviously I was wrong. You're so afraid of betrayal, you can't trust the instincts God gave you."

Tears gushed down Fran's cheeks. "You trusted your instincts, and look what happened to you."

Her mother shook her head helplessly. "Honey—you can't base your whole life on what happened to me!"

"But how did you stand it when you found out Daddy had been unfaithful?"

"It hurt, but it didn't ruin my life. If I found a man I could truly love, I'd risk it again."

Fran couldn't believe what she was hearing. "You really would get married again?"

"Of course. In fact I'm hoping it will happen, and wish it had happened when you were young so you could have seen what a good marriage was like. It was the abandoned child, not the grown-up woman, who couldn't get through the ceremony last night.

"Andre Benet must have an excess of all the husband potential you've been looking for, or you wouldn't have driven to Elko with him. You *do* love him."

"More than life itself," Fran whispered. "That's why I couldn't take it if he walked out on me, Mom."

Her mother got to her feet and stared piteously at Fran. "To live your whole life denying yourself happiness with a wonderful man in order to avoid something that in all probability will never happen, is the stuff real tragedies are made of.

"I wish I could help you, Fran. I love you so much." Her mother's voice trembled.

"I love you too."

"Under the circumstances, I'll tell Don and May you're too sick to come to dinner. We're due there in a few minutes."

"Thanks." Hot tears trickled down her cheeks. "I couldn't face anybody right now."

Mrs. Mallory gave her daughter a long hug. "Before you do anything else you need to call Howard and Barney so they won't worry."

Fran sniffed. "I will." She followed her mom to the door. They embraced one more time before they said goodbye.

Numb with pain, Fran stood paralyzed until she heard the phone ring. Her heart suddenly raced too hard. *Andre?*

She dashed into the kitchen to answer it. As soon as she said hello and heard Howard's voice, her heart plummeted. ''Fran?'' he repeated her name.

''Yes, Howard.'' She swallowed hard. ''I'm so glad you called here. I was just about to phone you. Mother came over to my house this morning and got me out of bed.'' The lies were beginning.

''I-I didn't realize you had already tried to reach me. I understand you came back to the party last night because your patient had gone into false labor. By then Andre had run me home. I'm so sorry everything went wrong.''

The prolonged silence on his end increased her pain. ''I'm not,'' came the unexpected response. ''Your involvement with Benet goes layers deep. Last night I realized I will never be in the running. That's why I've been trying to reach you, to wish you good luck. I mean that sincerely. But will you do me one favor?''

By now tears were dripping down her cheeks. ''Of course.''

''Don't stay away from church because of me. Since you never gave me the chance to suffer a broken heart, my bruised pride will mend soon enough. One day I hope to find a woman who loves me as much as you love Benet.''

When she could find her voice she said, ''You will, because you're a wonderful man. The very best,'' she said in a tortured whisper.

''Goodbye, Fran.''

Quick, before she broke down completely, she had to phone Barney.

To her relief, she reached his voice mail. She couldn't handle a conversation with him right now. After telling him the same lie she'd told Howard, she said she'd see him at the office in the morning, then hung up the phone and went back to bed. She wondered if there would ever be a reason to get out of it again.

The phone rang as Andre walked through the back door of his house. With the blood pounding in his ears he reached for the receiver in the kitchen. ''Francesca?''

''No.'' There was a slight hesitation. ''It's Natalie. I'm sorry,'' came the quiet apology.

Her call had the effect of ice water being thrown in his face. He tamped down hard on his disappointment. What a fool he was to think Francesca would phone him, but he was in pain. Today was supposed to be the first day of their honeymoon.

"Yes, Natalie? What can I do for you?"

Her only reason for phoning would have to be about business because when he'd said good-night to her last night, he'd let her know that he was in love with Francesca.

"Forgive me for the intrusion, especially after that fabulous party you gave last night. But you told me to call if a house came on the market that Gerda might like. I think I've found it. There's an open house going on right now."

He sucked in his breath. "I just got in, and their car isn't here. I would imagine they're at church. I don't expect them back until after four."

"That's too bad because I can tell you that even though it was just listed today, it will be gone by tonight. People kill for this location on the Avenues because it's near the university, yet has a wonderful view of the city.

"Amazingly, it's in Gerda's price range and not that far from your house. A one-family owner has kept it in mint condition, but because of financial problems, they have to move before Christmas. Do you want to meet me there?''

If this concerned anyone but Gerda, he would tell Natalie to call back later. But under the circumstances, he knew Gerda and her family were anxious to get settled in a place of their own. Maybe Natalie was right, and this was the house for them.

After spending part of the day at the monastery, he'd come up with a plan to pursue Francesca. Under the circumstances, the sooner he had his whole house to himself, the sooner he could carry out some ideas. Before long he intended to make her his wife. He couldn't wait to start a family. In fact he yearned for everything he'd been deprived of.

When the Judge had gotten to the part where Francesca was supposed to repeat her vows, Andre knew marriage was what he'd been starving for. He wasn't about to give up now.

``What's the address?''

``It's 823 Eleventh Avenue.''

``I'll be there in ten minutes. Thanks, Natalie.''

After leaving a note by the phone for Gerda explaining he'd gone house-hunting, he dressed in khakis and a polo shirt, then hurried out to his car. He didn't plan to be gone more than forty-five minutes at the most.

But in that assumption he was wrong. The place was packed with potential buyers, and the tour of the house took much longer than he had anticipated. As far as he could tell, it turned out to have everything Gerda had specified and more.

Afraid Natalie was right and it might get away from them if they didn't act fast, Andre wrote out a check for earnest money. It took Natalie a little while to finish her business with the other Realtor. By the time they went out to their cars, it was ten after four.

"Gerda ought to be home by the time I get there. Why don't you come over to the house. Then she and Harbin can follow you back here to see what they really think."

"That's a good idea. These papers are going to need her signature."

"Let's go."

Anxious to return to the house in case Francesca had broken down and phoned him, he drove faster than usual. To his relief, he saw Harbin's car parked in front.

Andre left his car in the driveway alongside the house and gestured to Natalie to stay in her car. Before he could put his key in the lock, the door opened. ''Andre!'' Gerda cried happily. ''I'm so glad you're home safe.''

He frowned. ''Why wouldn't I be? I left you a message.''

''I mean *before* you left your message.'' For the next few minutes Gerda explained about the frantic phone calls from everyone including Francesca's mother. ''No one could find either of you. That's when I began to worry you might have been in an accident.''

Lord.

''After what you've just told me, I have to go over to Francesca's apartment. I'll explain everything later, Gerda. Right now Natalie Cairns is waiting for you. She's found the perfect house for you in your price range. She was so excited about it, she asked me to check it out.

''I have to agree it's exactly what you've been looking for. We were both afraid it would be gone before the end of the day so I put earnest money down in case you wanted it.''

Gerda looked shocked. ''You used your own money?''

''You would have done the same for me, *ja?*''

The older woman's blue eyes misted over. ''*Ja.*''

''After everything we've been looking at for the last few weeks, it's a jewel, Gerda. I think all of you could be very happy there, and it's only a few minutes away from mine.''

''Thank you, Andre!'' Gerda cried fervently. ''Just today in church I prayed we would find a house soon. You are truly *mein Schatz.*''

''The feeling's mutual, Gerda. Now I've got to go.''

After making several errands, he sped all the way to Francesca's apartment complex. All he had going for him was the element of surprise. He planned to keep her so surprised, one day she would finally have to cave in.

It was almost six at night when Fran heard the doorbell ring. She wouldn't be at all surprised if it was her Uncle Donald. Though he was a dentist, he took care of everyone's minor medical needs in the family.

Assuming her mother had told him she was down with a cold or some such thing, she speculated he'd decided to run over and see if she needed an antibiotic. She loved him for being so good to her, but right now she wasn't in any shape to have company. She'd already swallowed a couple of painkillers, but her headache was still there big as life.

Although she'd taken a shower and had changed into a clean pair of navy sweats, nothing could repair the damage to her face after eight hours of nonstop sobbing. He would notice her puffy, red-rimmed eyes and unnatural pallor. In an instant he would ascertain her problems weren't medical.

With a towel still wrapped around her hair still damp from the shower, she walked over to the door. "Who's there?"

"Andre."

Her heart thudded sickeningly. He hadn't left town yet. Had he come to say goodbye?

She moaned, not wanting him to see her like this. But she didn't dare turn him away. There was so much she needed to say to him. First of all, she had to beg his forgiveness.

"Just a minute, Andre."

"Don't take too long or our food will get cold."

Food?

Without hesitating another instant, she undid the lock and opened the door. He stood there with a large bag in one arm. Her eyes traveled up the slate-blue polo shirt covering his well-defined chest, to the features of his arresting male face. When they reached his eyes, their gazes locked.

She'd never seen him look more attractive or beguiling. The impact of his presence robbed her of breath. If she hadn't backed out of their wedding at the last second, they'd be married now, enjoying their honeymoon.

Mortified by the way she must look to him, she told him to come in and put the food on the coffee table. "Give me a minute and I'll be right out."

"Take all the time you need. I'm not going anywhere."

If only that were true.

If only he could say that and mean it for the rest of their lives. No doubt her father had said it to her mother in the early stages of their marriage. Everybody said it, but not everybody meant it.

Her hands shook as she brushed her hair. She found a couple of combs and arranged it in a French twist. A little lipstick added some color. Maybe now he wouldn't recoil when he saw her.

By the time she went back to the living room, he'd turned on the TV and was watching a football game. He'd brought Chinese. It looked and smelled delicious. This morning she'd thought she'd never eat again, but twelve hours later she found she was hungry.

Stop lying to yourself, Fran. It's Andre's unexpected presence that has brought you back to life. Enjoy the moment for as long as it lasts because there won't be many more of them.

When she entered the room, his black eyes swept her body from head to toe. It caused her stomach to flutter. He had a way of making her feel beautiful even when she knew she wasn't looking her best.

"I like the way you've done your hair. You have lovely bones, Francesca."

She knew he was being sincere. Warmth seeped into her body. "Thank you, but I take no credit. They're one of my mother's many contributions."

"I'm looking forward to meeting her." He levered himself from the chair. "Come and sit down. I've made a plate for you. Since I don't know your taste in Chinese yet, I brought us a little of everything." He handed her the food and a can of Coke.

"Thank you." She took them from him, but couldn't eat. He spoke as if they were a couple with a future ahead of them. How could he behave like this after what she'd done to him?

"Andre— About last nigh—"

"Last night was my fault," he interjected in a forbidding voice before swallowing some of his drink. "I take full responsibility for coercing you into something you weren't ready for."

Her chest heaved. "I thought I was ready to marry you. I'm so sorry for hurting you."

His dark eyes impaled her. "Francesca— No apology is necessary. Because of my impatience to be your husband, I rushed you off your feet. I wanted you so badly, I didn't listen to you in my study when you said you couldn't make a decision about marrying me in a matter of minutes.

"The fact is, last night I relied on the strong physical chemistry between us to win you around. But it was wrong of me. We need time to get to know each other like this before we marry."

She shook her head and got to her feet. "You don't understand, Andre. Time isn't going to make any difference." *Spending more time with you is going to make me fall deeper in love. I can't afford to let that happen.*

While they'd been talking, she'd watched him consume all his food including the last egg roll. "That's your fear talking. We'll just take it a day at a time. Right now that's about all I can handle." His words sounded slightly slurred.

"Andre? Are you all right?"

His eyes had closed. "I haven't been to bed since night before last. Would you mind if I just sat here on your couch for a minute before I go?"

Before Fran could fathom it, he'd gone to sleep. She could tell by the deep, even tenor of his breathing.

It didn't really surprise her. Not only had he given a huge party, he'd done all the driving last night. Combine that with the emotional trauma they'd both been through and it wasn't surprising that he would suddenly collapse in her living room.

With her compassion at the forefront, she went in search of bedding for him. "Come on, Andre," she whispered seconds later. "Lie down." With a gentle nudge he did as he was told, and she covered him with a quilt. He made a contented sound and stretched a little as if to find a more comfortable position.

She could see he was so far gone he had no idea what was happening. Unable to resist, she sank to her knees to look at him. He appeared more vulnerable in repose. His long black lashes curled at the tips against the slight flush of his hard-boned cheeks. She could detect the shadow of his beard around his firm jaw. If she touched it with her fingertips like she was longing to do, it might waken him.

His mother had bequeathed him all that black, curly hair and olive skin. With a straight nose and compelling mouth reminiscent of the Abbot's, there wasn't anything about him that wasn't perfect to her.

If she were his wife, she would have the right to lie there with him this very instant. She yearned to kiss him until she'd aroused his passion. Just watching him like this kindled the ache inside of her to know his possession.

Her gaze traveled over his strong, virile body. One bronzed, sinewy arm lay loose on top of the quilt. He'd done a lot of hard physical work in his life to be in such amazing shape. Though Andre felt his life was so different from his father's, Fran could see many similarities.

The monks were renowned for performing hard physical labor from early morning till nightfall. When they weren't active, they studied. Andre had purchased books on every subject imaginable. He'd obtained a university education she still wanted to hear about.

When she thought of the many places all over the earth he must have visited, she longed to hear about his adventures, especially those at sea. In truth, she wanted to know about every fascinating detail of his life before they'd met.

He was so different from other males of her acquaintance. Men like Howard were blessed with a constant male role model from the cradle. Andre had no masculine influence to teach him who he was, no siblings. Yet in spite of it all, he had grown into a spectacular man of superior intellect and sophisticated tastes.

His aunt had everything to do with that. As far as Fran was concerned, she'd done a superb job. Andre's kindness to Gerda, his faultless manners spoke of a priceless education which had to have been learned at his aunt's knee.

But when a boy grew into his teens, he needed other men. It was no mystery why Andre had gone to sea. He'd been in Turkey of all places when he'd first heard his aunt was dying.

If he hadn't made it to her sickbed in time, he would never have known that his father was alive and living in Salt Lake. Andre wouldn't be lying here on the couch right now where Fran could feast her eyes on him to her heart's content.

How strange that it had been Paul's assignment to go out to the monastery, yet circumstances had forced Fran to conduct the interview instead.

That fateful meeting with Andre had changed her whole life. He *was* her whole life. But if she married him and then he left her, it would destroy her.

As if she was suddenly too close to a roaring fire, she forced herself to get up and back away from him. Needing something physical to do, she took all the mess out to the kitchen.

Though she hadn't been hungry before, now she devoured what was left of the tasty food. After she'd eaten and brushed her teeth, she turned out lights and went to bed. She had no idea when Andre would wake up, probably not until she'd dressed and left for work in the morning.

But in that assessment, she was wrong. When she emerged from her bedroom at seven having enjoyed a surprisingly good sleep, she saw the folded quilt on the table with the pillow. Evidently Andre had awakened some time during the night and had slipped out of the apartment before her alarm had sounded.

She hated the hollow feeling that always attacked her when she knew he'd gone off. In an effort to counteract the sensation, she went into the kitchen to make toast and pour herself some orange juice. Thank goodness it was a Monday morning. She could wish this one would be hellishly busy so she wouldn't be tortured by thoughts of him.

Forty-five minutes later she walked into the office. Something was different the second she started back toward her desk. Her eyes zeroed in on a breathtaking arrangement of long-stemmed red roses which dwarfed her desk....

"Three dozen of them," Paul quipped. "I counted."

They had the largest heads and were the most beautiful, fragrant flowers she'd ever seen in her life. Her pulse went crazy.

"Hey—don't just stand there like a zombie. There's the card."

"D-Did you see who brought them?"

"A delivery man."

"But it's too early for floral deliveries."

"Evidently not this time." He grinned. "Come on, Frannie. Don't keep me in suspense, or do you want me to open the card for you?''

She bit her lip and looked away. ''I think I know who sent them.''

''Everyone around here is betting on the monk.''

''That's not funny, Paul. For one thing, he's not a monk.''

''Hey—I was only kidding. You must really be wacko about this guy to be so touchy this morning.''

I almost married him night before last. That's how wacko I am.

She saw that *Francesca* had been written on the outside of the envelope. No one called her by her full name except Andre.

When she picked it up, she realized it wasn't flat. Something was inside it besides the card. With pounding heart, she slit the top with her letter opener, then gasped when the gold ring fell onto her desk pad.

Paul let out a low whistle. ''Ladies and gentlemen. Will you look at that.''

She picked it up and folded it in her palm. What was Andre thinking?

Gingerly, she drew out the card and read it.

My darling—
Forgive me for falling asleep on you last night. Was I mistaken or did an angel watch over me while I slept?

Wear this ring around your neck until you're ready to let me put it on your finger. Perhaps if my father had asked the same thing of my mother, they would have spent their lives together instead of apart.

I love you, Francesca.

Andre.

Paul thrust a box of tissues under her nose. "Go ahead. Use as many as you like. Just tell me one thing— Can I announce that you're officially engaged now?"

"No, Paul!" she cried in fresh anguish. "You don't understand. Please don't say a word about this ring to a soul."

He sobered. "All right. My lips are sealed."

"Thank you."

"But you love the guy. I know you do."

"I don't deny it," she whispered heatedly. The ring seemed to burn a brand into her skin.

"Frannie— Not every man out there is a freak of nature. It might surprise you to know that a lot of men are monogamous by choice!"

"I know. You're one of them."

"It looks to me like the sailor man has heard your siren's call. Now he has washed up on your shore. Is it going to be to his doom, Frannie baby?"

"Oh, Paul."

She shook her head in exasperation and despair. The tears won out. Her shoulders started to shake.

"Uh-oh. Here comes Barney."

She grabbed another tissue and wiped her eyes.

"Well, well, well. What do we have here?"

Slowly she turned around to face her boss. Without looking at him she said, "Roses from a friend."

"Anyone I know?"

"They're from Andre."

"I would say so. They have his stamp written all over them. You've pulled off a major coup. It's too bad I'm going to have to send you on that assignment to Washington D.C.

today. But the rest of us will enjoy his gift while you're away."

"*What assignment?*" She forgot not to look him in the eye.

"You remember the issue we're doing in the spring about Utahans away from Utah?"

"Yes, of course." It was a lie. She'd forgotten all about it. Andre's advent in her life had turned everything upside down.

"I've just received permission for you to interview our congressmen. They want you to come this week while they're still in legislative session. Next week it will be adjourned for Christmas. Now's our opportunity."

A week away from home... Would Andre still be here when she got back?

"This won't be a political piece. We want to give the readers a close-up look at our elected officials going through the daily grind in our nation's capitol. Most people have no idea what the insides of their offices look like, let alone their hourly schedules. I'm convinced personal interviews with their secretaries and aides will give you the kind of copy we're looking for.

"Since this is such late notice, you're free to go home now and get ready. Stop by Emily's desk on the way out. She has your airline tickets and hotel reservation. Your flight leaves at eleven."

So soon?

"Hey—' Barney smiled. "I was only kidding about keeping the flowers here."

"I'll help her out with them," Paul offered "Come on, Frannie. You've got to hustle."

Like a sleepwalker, she put the ring in her purse, then followed Paul through the office to Emily's desk for her travel documents.

For the first time she could remember, she didn't want to go on assignment. She didn't want to go anywhere. But business was business.

The second she got home she put water back in the vase and placed the roses on her coffee table. They were so breathtaking she couldn't take her eyes off of them.

She phoned her mother to tell her about her plans and ask her to check on her apartment while she was away.

After she put down the receiver, she debated what to do about Andre. She couldn't leave

Salt Lake without acknowledging his gift. Since she had no intention of keeping the ring, she decided she would drive by his house and give it to him in person. That way she could thank him for the flowers at the same time.

When he answered his door twenty minutes later, fresh-shaven and dressed in jeans and a charcoal turtleneck, she had to fight with herself not to stare at him like she'd done last night while he was asleep.

''Good morning,'' he murmured huskily, his eyes playing over her upturned features with heartthrobbing intensity. ''I'd hoped to see you later in the day. To find you on my doorstep this early is a pleasure I hadn't anticipated. Come in.''

''I-I can't, Andre. I'm on my way to the airport.''

Lines darkened his face as he straightened from a lounging position. ''You've been sent on an assignment?''

''Yes. Washington D.C. I just stopped by for a minute to thank you for the magnificent ros—''

''Why don't we talk about that while I drive you to the airport in my car. I'll keep yours here in the garage where it will be safe until you get back.''

She protested on a small moan. ''Much as I appreciate the offer, I don't want to put you out, Andre. You've done more than you should already.''

''If you recall,'' he reminded her with an edge to his tone, ''you told me when we got back from Elko that you wanted me to do what *I* wanted to do. Did I misunderstand you?''

She averted her eyes from his piercing regard. ''No, but I didn't mean that you should wait on me hand and foot either.''

''I like doing things for you. It fills my life with purpose. Come in for a moment while I grab my keys and wallet from the bedroom. Then we'll go.''

Against her better judgement, she stepped inside and once again found herself awed by the charm of his home, not to mention the fabulous furnishings he'd purchased throughout his many travels.

He slid his arm around her shoulders and drew her close. ''Let's go in the living room where you'll be more comfortable,'' he whispered against her temple.

As they walked, their hips and thighs brushed intimately together. She feared he could feel the quaking of her body.

"Oh—" Fran let out a hushed cry when she caught sight of Natalie Cairns walking toward them. She had no idea he had company. "Hello, Mrs. Cairns."

"Good morning," the other woman said brightly.

"Look, Andre— Obviously you're busy, so—"

"Not at all," he said in a smooth tone, still holding her fast. "Natalie is here to see Gerda. Darling, did I tell you the Richters have bought a house and will be moving into it before Christmas?"

"No. I didn't know that." It meant Andre would be alone again. Her heart sank to her feet. How long would he stay in Salt Lake once Gerda and her family were settled elsewhere? "That's wonderful," she muttered because something was expected of her.

"I can hear Gerda coming down the stairs now," Natalie said. "Nice to see both of you again."

CHAPTER NINE

ANDRE LISTENED FOR their footsteps until he heard the front door close. "I don't know about you, but I have to have *this,* or I won't be able to function." He pulled Francesca into his arms, needing her kiss like he needed air to breathe.

"No, Andre!" she blurted, trying to avoid his mouth while she pushed her hands against his chest. "We don't have time. Besides, I-I can't think when you touch me, and there's something I need to talk to you about."

He continued to rain kisses along the side of her neck, his arms still holding her. "I don't want you to think. That's when you get into trouble," he whispered the words in a teasing tone.

She hid her face from him. "Please, Andre," she said, her voice trembling. "This is serious. It's about your ring. I can't accept it."

With the greatest of reluctance he removed his hands. As soon as he let go of her, she reached in her purse for the gold band and handed it back to him.

Her eyes pleaded with him for understanding. "I can't marry you, Andre. Since it's such a precious heirloom, I wouldn't dare keep it in my possession."

She backed further away from him and clung to one of the chairs, as if she needed to put up a shield between them. Andre realized she required special handling. He just hadn't planned on things getting difficult quite this soon.

"I'm sorry I behaved the way I did in front of Natalie Cairns. I thou—"

"I know exactly what construction you put on her presence here," he finished the sentence for her. "If I had felt that way about Natalie, I would never have pursued you.

"As it is, I'm in love with you. I've told her and everyone else in this house that you're my fiancée. Gerda and her family realize that you have every right to come and go here as you please. One day this is going to be your house too."

She finally met his gaze. Her startled green eyes mirrored her confusion. ''But I'm *not* your fiancée.''

''You are as far as I'm concerned. Did you ever get hold of Dr. Barker?''

His question seemed to throw her. ''Yes.''

''Though I can't imagine it, did he get ugly?''

She shook her silky blond head. ''No. Howard said he realized I was in love with you. He even—'' Her throat was working.

''What?'' Andre prodded.

''He asked me not to stay away from church because of him.''

''As I told you earlier, he's a good man.''

''He is.''

''But he's not the man for you, *thank God.* Come on, darling. If we're going to get you to the airport on time, we need to transfer your things to my car.''

Without giving her a chance to protest, he ushered her from the room and walked her through the house to get his keys.

''What happened when you talked to your mother?'' he asked minutes later when they were in his car, backing down the drive. "Does she know we almost got married?"

Francesca hugged her corner of the seat. "Yes."

Andre was elated over that fact. "Judging from your reaction, I take it she'll never be able to forgive me for attempting to elope with her daughter. No doubt she wants nothing to do with me."

"That's not true," she said in a shaky voice. "She would like to meet you. As for our not getting married, she was...disappointed."

"Francesca—if that's the case, then let's plan another wedding. We'll keep it a secret until you're ready for everyone to know."

"No, Andre. In the first place my mother wouldn't consider us married if we did that."

"What do you mean?"

She moistened her lips, a habit she didn't seem to be aware of when she was nervous. "I know her views. She would say that a marriage kept in the dark is no marriage, and that all we've done is get a license to—to—"

"Indulge our pleasure?" Andre easily supplied the words she couldn't speak. "Your mother's right. A bride is supposed to shout her happiness to the world.

"My Aunt Maudelle wanted me to get married so badly, I believe she'd already designed the wedding dress for my intended before I ever left New Orleans."

After a pause, "Were you in love with a girl in your teens?"

Her curiosity made Andre smile inwardly. "No, but my aunt had several choice young ladies picked out for me. Good Catholic girls from fine French families with impeccable pedigrees."

"She certainly wouldn't have approved of me then."

He chuckled. "By the time I turned thirty, if I had brought you home to meet her with my ring on your finger, she would have bowed down and kissed your Protestant feet for joy."

"I think my mother has reached that point herself."

"Since she's still very much alive, then maybe we ought to consider doing something to make us all happy."

"Andre— I'd rather we changed the subject."

"I think not. We need to talk about your fears and deal with them. From all accounts you've been raised in a God-fearing home by a wonderful woman who lived through your father's betrayal and is still anxious for you to marry."

"But it's so unfair what happened to her!"

"I agree."

"My father came from a prominent family with a wonderful pedigree. He was educated and had every opportunity to succeed. He and Mother fell madly in love. According to my grandmother, everyone said it was the match of the decade.

"A few years after they'd been married, he started to travel. Pretty soon he was gone weekends, then whole weeks at a time. At an early age, I can remember hearing my mother cry at night. I knew why, because I was crying for him too."

She turned her head to look at him. Those green orbs glittered with unshed tears. "How can anyone know what the future is going to hold? Uncle Donald, my father's brother, is just the opposite. He's a rock, devoted to his wife and children.

"What went wrong with my father? How could he have done what he did to Mother and me?" Her voice quivered.

Andre's jaw hardened. Francesca's fears went soul deep. For the first time in their relationship he began to wonder if there was any hope for them.

"I don't have an answer for that, Francesca. No one does. All you can do is try to live your own life to the fullest. That's what I want to do. *With you.*"

"Until you grow tired of me?" She fired the question at him.

"That works both ways," he said struggling to stay on an even keel with her. "But in our case we're older than some couples. Having found each other a little later in life, I don't see our feelings changing for each other. When the children come, it will only put a seal on our love."

"What if we don't have children?"

With her head bent, he wasn't certain he'd heard her correctly. "Is there a medical reason why you can't have them?"

Her head flew back. "No. But what if one of us decided we didn't want them?"

"Well, probably not for a little while after our marriage. Right now I can't think beyond making love to you for days and nights on end."

"Andre—" came her anguished cry. "Do you really want children?"

Her question surprised him. Maybe it shouldn't have, but it did. "Of course. One of the reasons I bought the house is because it has five spacious bedrooms. I was hoping we'd fill them with some golden-haired cherubs and a few little dark-eyed boys. But not all in one day."

"That's really one of your dreams?" she asked, her voice shaking.

He studied her appealing features for a moment, wondering what was going on inside that lovely head of hers. "I grew up with an aunt who never knew the love of a man. She was cross most of the time.

"For company, I hung around my friends and their families. Was it any wonder that I often found myself dreaming about belonging to a family of my own with a loving mother and father and a bunch of brothers and sisters who could still play with me after my friends had to go home?''

His response seemed to have stunned her.

''Francesca— What's wrong?''

''I may have had dreams like that and don't remember. All I know is that when my father left us, I made up my mind never to marry or have children.''

He pursed his lips. ''I would imagine most children would feel that way if they'd lived through your experience. Thankfully you grew up to be the breathtaking woman I want for my wife. When the time is right, we'll have children, and we'll love them all.''

''But what if that time never comes?''

Her question, painful for him, reached down into his soul.

''You see why I couldn't go through with the ceremony the other night?'' she blurted. ''When the Judge talked about children, I couldn't make the promise to put your happiness before mine by bearing you children. If anything happened to our love, at least we'd only hurt each other.''

The car resounded with her muffled sobs. She finally lifted her head. ''We're approaching the terminal. Please let me out at the curb. I don't want you to come in with me. Promise me, Andre.''

After what she'd just revealed, he was in no mood to upset her further. There was a lot he needed to sort out when he was alone. After braking several times, he pulled over to the side. ''Before you get out, let me leave you with this.''

He reached behind her neck and pulled her close to kiss her. ''I'm going to go out of my mind while you're gone. You're my life, Francesca—the only thing that matters,'' he murmured feverishly against her mouth. ''Surely by now you know that. I'll be here waiting for you when you fly home.''

A shadow darkened her eyes, as if she wanted to believe him but couldn't trust him to keep his word. What would it take to make the shadows go away forever?

''I love you, Andre,'' she cried passionately before responding to his kiss with an urgency that made him feel reborn.

As long as he had *this,* he could be patient in his greed for all the other things he wanted from her. He thought he'd learned patience at sea. But after meeting Francesca, he realized he didn't know the meaning of the word.

"We thank thee for this beautiful new house in this beautiful city. We thank thee for leading us to this wonderful country and this wonderful church. Most of all, we thank thee for our beloved friend, Andre, who has been so good to us.

"He is truly a saint and deserves all of heaven's blessings. Please watch over him and let him know we will always consider him to be a part of our family. And now we ask thee to bless this food, that it will nourish and strengthen our bodies. Help us to do good in thy service. Amen."

"Amen," Andre murmured, his eyes smarting. He was touched by Gerda's heartfelt prayer. It felt good to sit around the table with their family in their new home and see how happy they were. Only one thing was missing. One person…

While Harbin carved the beef tenderloin roast he seemed to read Andre's mind. "When will Ms. Mallory be back?"

''Late tonight. The blizzards are worse in the east than they are here. Her flight kept getting delayed, but the last time I called, her plane had finally left Logan airport.''

Gerda eyed him compassionately. ''I'm sorry it has been such a long wait, Andre. I know how much you are missing her.''

''She's my life.''

One of her eyebrows flexed. ''Then you must do something about it.''

It was the first time Gerda had ever preached to him where Francesca was concerned. For a moment she reminded him of his Aunt Maudelle.

The time for truth had come. He captured her loving gaze. ''I intend to. As soon as she gets off the plane.''

The waiting had been hell. Their nightly phone calls weren't enough.

''*Ja?*'' she asked in a wondering voice.

''You remember the night of the party?''

''Of course. Who could forget such a magnificent time?''

''I agree. It came close to being the most magnificent night of my life. Francesca and I drove to Nevada. We almost got married.''

Gerda's smile faded. ''What do you mean, almost?''

''She backed out during the ceremony.''

Everyone at the table gasped.

''It's all right. She's had some fears to conquer. Tonight I have a plan to help her.''

''Why didn't you tell me? You've been in pain.''

''Francesca is very fragile. I didn't want her to think anyone else knew about it.''

Gerda frowned. ''But why would she want to back out of marriage with you? You're so wonderful!''

''I love your exaggerations, Gerda. But thank you just the same. As for Francesca, she has her reasons.''

''No reason could be good enough to prevent her from marrying you. I've been waiting to give you a big wedding party.''

''I can't think of anything nicer. When Francesca is ready, we'll both come to you to arrange something.''

''So tonight is the night?''

''Yes.''

I'm delighted for you, Andre.'' She clapped her hands. ''Soon there will be little Andres running about your beautiful house. You think you are happy now. Just wait until you hold your first child in your arms.''

Harbin's blue eyes gleamed. ''Mother's right, Andre. A house truly becomes a home when the little ones arrive.''

''I must admit I'm looking forward to that day myself. But right now I'd settle to have Francesca back safely back in my arms.''

''Of course you would,'' she commiserated.

''After dinner, *if* you think you can concentrate, we'll continue our chess game until you have to leave for the airport,'' Harbin suggested.

Andre flashed him a smile. ''You wouldn't by any chance be planning to take advantage of me would you?''

''Ja.'' A big grin broke out on Harbin's face.

''I don't mind. I need the distraction.''

''I thought you might.''

An hour later Harbin declared checkmate. Andre's thoughts had definitely not been on the game. He thanked the family for their hospitality, then left the house and headed for the airport.

The streets had been plowed, making it easier to maneuver the Mercedes. Thank heaven he wouldn't be going home alone tonight. Now that Gerda's family had moved out, the place felt deserted. He needed Francesca to give it life, to fill it with love.

Fran stared out of the jet's window into the darkness. Now that the pilot had announced the approach for Salt Lake International Airport, she was feeling sick to her stomach. Andre was down there waiting for her.

The long, desolately lonely week punctuated with phone calls that only made the aching worse, had proven one thing to her. He was too exceptional a man to hurt.

He wanted children, a family. Fran could give him love, but she couldn't give him those things. She refused.

For that reason she would tell him it was truly over. Tonight she had to walk away from him while she was still strong enough.

It had been a mistake to drive to Nevada and raise his hopes. The night of the party she had thought with her heart instead of her head. Thank heavens they hadn't slept together.

Even so, she was in the kind of emotional trouble she might never get out of if she didn't sever the bond immediately.

It wasn't too late. They'd only been seeing each other off and on since his party. Compared to marriage of a year or five year's duration, a week or so was nothing.

Andre wouldn't fight her on this. He wanted children. That fact had come across loud and clear on their drive to the airport. When he knew there was no hope, he would disappear from Salt Lake forever. That was what she wanted. It was the only way she would survive.

Since the first day she'd set eyes on him, her life had been nothing but an exercise in agony. He'd represented forbidden fruit, something she hadn't been able to resist. Now having dared to taste it, she would be required to suffer over the loss.

Whoever said it was better to have loved and lost than never to have loved at all—They'd never fallen under the spell of Andre Benet. They didn't have the faintest conception of what they were talking about.

"Francesca? Over here, darling."

Even before she spotted him in the crowd of passengers assembled in the terminal waiting room, she could hear the deep resonance in his voice calling to her.

The second she saw his handsome face she averted her eyes, refusing to indulge herself when she planned to end their relationship as soon as possible.

He reached for her and clung. "I thought this day would never come. Let's get out of here." She could feel his urgency to be alone with her, but because of the press from the crowd he didn't try to kiss her. It was her salvation for the moment—another chance to harden herself for what was to come.

After relieving her of her camera case, he slid his hand to her neck and ushered her downstairs to retrieve her luggage and briefcase. Fran was afraid to talk until they had complete privacy. Andre must have felt the same way. Instead of verbal conversation, his fingers caressed her skin, sending a silent message that soon they would be alone to welcome each other in the only way that could assuage their needs. Though she tried not to react, his touch set off prickles of delight throughout her body.

After the freezing cold of the carpark, Fran detected a lingering warmth in the Mercedes as Andre helped her inside and shut the door. When he had taken his place behind the wheel, he started the engine, then reached across the console to take her in his arms.

"You've been away too long," he murmured in an aching voice.

It was agony not to respond, but she was fighting for her life. Turning her head to the side to avoid his mouth she said, "Andre? Would you mind just driving me home? I'm not feeling very well at the moment. I'll get my car from your house later."

She felt his slight hesitation before his hands slowly released her and he sat back in the leather seat. Out of the periphery she could tell his dark, intelligent eyes were studying her intently. "When we last spoke, you didn't sound ill. Did you get airsick?"

"No," she answered, her voice trembling.

"Then you must have come down with a cold. It's a good thing you're back so I can take care of you."

No, Andre— her heart cried in renewed anguish. *I can't let you do that. I can't let myself become any more vulnerable to you than I already am.*

In an economy of movement he turned up the heat and reversed the car so they could exit the parking area with dispatch. By the time they joined the freeway leading into the city, Fran felt the necessity of making some sort of conversation to ease the palpable tension inside the car.

"I-It looks like Salt Lake's streets are in better shape than those back east."

She heard him suck in his breath. "Obviously something happened while you've been away to turn you inside out. Don't play games with me, Francesca. We've been through too much together not to tell each other the truth. I want to know what's wrong, and I want to know it now."

She'd had enough experience around Andre to realize he always meant what he said. But she felt it would be better if he weren't driving when she broached the subject of ending their relationship.

"Could we at least pull off to the side of the road then?"

He flashed her a look she couldn't decipher. "In other words, whatever it is you have to say to me might cause me to lose control of the car."

Fran shook her head in despair. "No, Andre— I just prefer to talk at the apartment."

"I thought you wanted to go home."

"I do."

"Your home is with me now. I'm not asking you to sleep with me. Only to live under the same roof with me for a while, to get used to the idea. Gerda's family is installed in their new house. There's nothing to prevent us from being together now."

She couldn't look at him. "Yes, there is."

"Francesca— I've given it a great deal of thought." He went on speaking as if she hadn't said anything. "If you don't want children, so be it. Without you, there's no point to anything. You and I can have an incredible life just as we are."

No, Andre. No.

She shook her head. "I can't ask you to sacrifice for me that way."

‘‘Why?’’ he demanded. ‘‘Have I suddenly grown another head?’’ His voice was icily mocking. He sounded so different from the man she thought she knew, her alarm grew.

‘‘Please don’t talk like that, not even in jest.’’

‘‘If you think I was jesting, then you don’t know me at all.’’

‘‘Andre—’’ In her agitation she nervously rubbed her hands against her thighs. She could tell he was aware of her every movement. It increased her anxiety until she thought she might jump out of her skin. Finally she found the courage to say the words.

‘‘I’ve made the decision not to see you again.’’

After that revelation, she didn’t know what to expect. But she hadn’t counted on the absolute quiet coming from Andre’s side of the car.

He continued to drive as if he hadn’t heard what she said. At first she thought he would take her to his house whether she wanted to go there or not. But when they passed by the turnoff for the northeast area of the city, she realized he intended to drive her to the apartment as she had requested.

She tortured the straps of her purse. "Please, Andre—say something."

The speed of the car didn't change. Neither did his facial features which revealed a mask-like appearance in the shadowy light. "I think you've said it all."

Her mouth had gone so dry she could hardly articulate. "Our relationship has been a mistake from the beginning. We were both carried away by our passion, but those fiery emotions won't last forever. It will be easier if we end it now and go our own way."

When there was nothing forthcoming from his end, she began to panic. "While I was in Washington D.C., I had time to do a lot of thinking in my hotel room every night too. You've been leading an unnatural life here in Salt Lake. Be honest, Andre. You love the sea.

"The only reason you came out West was because of your father. Now that he's gone, there's nothing to hold you. I've been a distraction, that's all."

Now that she'd started this, she couldn't seem to stop. "I'm the one who flirted with you that first day when I had no business doing any such thing. Even though you weren't a monk, I had no way of knowing that; yet I purposely provoked you into paying attention to me because I was so attracted to you. It was wrong of me."

She struggled for breath. "I hope that one day you can forgive me for being such a terrible person, for telling you I would marry you when I knew deep in my heart it wouldn't work. You need to do what makes you happy. After the adventurous life you've led, you'll die of suffocation in Salt Lake."

Still he said nothing as they turned onto her street.

"I have no intention of marrying, but eventually I know you'll find a woman who can give you all the things you need, all the things you deserve. No one deserves a perfect marriage and children more than you do. I wish I could be that woman to give you those things, but I can't. *I can't,*" she said in a tortured whisper.

"I believe you," he said gratingly. They'd pulled up to the curb in front of her apartment building. "There were men at sea like you, emotionally crippled from childhood, unable to lead full lives. The damage had gone too deep at too young an age. Some psychiatrists call it a brain breeze. No one can help them. You're obviously one of those people.''

Fran sat there stunned by his words, let alone his civilized acceptance of the situation. He got out of the car and proceeded to pull her cases from the trunk. The next thing she knew he had opened the door on the passenger side to help her through the snow.

Andre had always been a gentleman, but this display of manners when she knew he was in so much pain, was intolerable.

''Please, Andre. I can make it inside with my things.''

''I have no doubt of it. A woman still single at twenty-eight years of age has learned how to fend for herself. But since I'm here and willing, why not take advantage of me. After I'm gone, you can revel in your single status to your heart's content.''

A stabbing pain in her heart sent a shock wave through her body, almost immobilizing her.

He started for the building. She had no choice but to follow him through the entry and down the hall to her door.

''I'll have your car delivered to you first thing in the morning.''

Quick before she collapsed, Fran fumbled in her purse for the key and inserted it in the lock. Andre was right behind her. The minute she heard the click, he opened the door and placed her bags inside the minuscule foyer.

Before she could credit it, he'd made a tour of her apartment. ''Everything seems to be in order,'' he stated equably as he reappeared in the front hall seconds later.

For a brief interval she felt his dark gaze sweep over her face and body, but his eyes were veiled, hiding his thoughts.

''More than anyone else, a sailor understands about two ships passing in the night.

''With a dark, bottomless, pitiless sea all around them, they feel a temporary connection, a little link of humanity to humanity until both disappear into the void in opposite directions, never to pass each other again.

''For one sweet, shining moment, we linked, you and I. Believe it or not, I consider myself one of the lucky ones who can go off with that memory in my heart. Some mortals are destined never to come close.

"Goodbye, Francesca."

She swayed and had to catch hold of the door jamb so she wouldn't fall.

This wasn't like any of the other times.

This time he wouldn't show up again unexpectedly.

This time it was really over.

Andre Benet had just walked out of her life.

He can never hurt you now.

He's gone for good.

You can get back to the life you were leading before you drove out to that monastery and entered forbidden territory.

"Natalie?"

"Andre?"

"Yes. Forgive me for calling you this late, but it's important."

"Please don't apologize. It goes with the job. Besides, I consider you a good friend. You can bother me any time you want. Is everything all right at the Richters?"

"When I left them at dinner a few hours ago, they were beaming. I have a feeling they'll be able to take root in a house like that. But they're not the reason I'm calling."

"How can I help you?"

"I'm leaving Salt Lake later tonight. I won't be coming back."

"What?" She gasped. "But I thoug—"

"Natalie— just hear me out. I've packed the things I'm going to take with me. Everything else can be sold with the house. I'm leaving the sale of it in your capable hands. You've already worked with my lawyer. Contact him when you have a buyer. He has the power of attorney to act for me and will invest the money."

"But Andre—"

"There are things you don't know, Natalie. Please continue to be my friend and carry out my wishes. That's all I ask."

"Of course I will," she responded in a subdued voice. "I'll get top price for you."

"I never doubted it. Thank you for everything. I'll always be grateful for your help. You're the best at what you do. Take care, Natalie."

Andre only had two more things to do before he left for the airport. After pulling a sheet of paper from his bureau drawer, he began his letter in German.

Dear Gerda—

You've been like a mother to me. Tonight I'm writing to you as a son.

Francesca has turned me down. I understand her reasons, but I can no longer live in this city, let alone this country.

You may not hear from me for a long time, but always know I will cherish you and your family in my heart.

I'm leaving you my car as a housewarming gift. This way you and Harbin won't have to share his. It's German-made, so I trust you won't disapprove. My attorney will be contacting you to change the title and give you the key.

If things could only work out for one of us, I'm glad it was you. You're one of the noble of the earth. It has been a privilege to know you and your family. May you always be happy, Gerda.

I hope that when you think of me, you

will refer to me as your *schatz*. I'm very attached to the appellation.

All my love,

Andre.

He folded the letter and put it in an envelope. When he arrived at the airport, he would post it.

Forty-five minutes later he told the taxi driver to follow Francesca's car while he drove it over to her apartment complex. After dropping her key in the mailbox, he got in the taxi. Ten minutes after that he asked the driver to wait for him in the monastery parking lot.

It was after midnight. The brothers would all be asleep by now. He didn't need a light as he made his way around the back of the monastery. Many were the nights he found himself standing at the foot of his father's grave when he couldn't sleep.

Tonight was such a night with one enormous difference.

"I couldn't leave without telling you something that should bring you great solace. It was here in Salt Lake that I met a woman and found the meaning of life. You don't have to worry about me anymore. Rest in peace, Father."

CHAPTER TEN

"HELLO? GERDA?"

After a brief silence, "Is that you, Francesca?"

"Yes. Please forgive me for disturbing you."

"You're not disturbing me, my dear. I'm very happy to hear your voice."

"It's good to talk to you too. Gerda? I went over to the house a few minutes ago and saw a For Sale sign on Andre's property. No one answered the door. Do you know where he is? I need to talk to him."

Again Fran heard the hesitation coming from the older woman. "He sent us a letter. It said that he had gone away and wouldn't be back."

"Where did he go, Gerda?" she cried. "I have to find him!"

"I wish I knew."

Gerda sounded too sincere to be lying. "Do you think Natalie Cairns would have any idea?"

"No. I already asked her. She's handling the sale of Andre's house. Apparently he told her to sell everything, even the furnishings."

Dear God. *What have I done?*

"I also spoke to Mr. Earl, Andre's attorney," Gerda murmured. "If he knows where Andre is, he's been told not to divulge that information to anyone."

Fran moaned. "It's my fault Andre went away."

"He has loved you for a very long time."

"Oh, Gerda. I love him so much you can't possibly imagine. I've got to find him!"

"I agree the situation is desperate. Perhaps if you inquired at the monastery."

The monastery.

"I think you were inspired. He wouldn't leave without saying goodbye to them. I'm going to drive over there right now."

"Let me know if you hear anything. Naturally I will phone you if I should have word of his whereabouts."

"Thank you."

"There's no need to thank me. We both love him, *ja*?"

"Oh yes!"

But half an hour later, Fran's hopes for a lead were dashed when Brother Joseph in the gift shop could shed no light.

"I'm in love with him, Brother Joseph. Maybe he didn't tell you about us, but he loves me too. I just want to find him and talk to him. He asked me to marry him. I want to tell him yes."

The older priest eyed her with compassion. "I didn't know. Congratulations. It would have made the Abbot very happy."

"I sincerely hope so. The only problem is, Andre and I had a misunderstanding and now I'm desperate to find him. Don't you have any idea where he might be? Didn't he share anything with you?"

"No, I'm sorry."

"If you do hear something, could you let me know?"

"Come back in a week. Perhaps there will be some word."

"Yes. I'll do that. Thank you," she said and turned quickly away, afraid she would burst into tears right in front of him.

She made it as far as the door when he called her back. "There's a postcard here for him. It came a few days ago. Since you're planning to marry him, perhaps you'd like to take it with you."

Curious to know who would be writing him, she took it from the monk and read the message.

Dear Andre—

The wife and I have thought it over. If you don't think your sweetheart will mind, we'd love to come to Salt Lake and stay with you in your new house. Frankly, I can't wait to see it.

But it will have to be the day after Christmas because we're spending Christmas Day with her folks.

Here's my phone number. Just give me a call and we'll make final arrangements. The kids can't wait to ski with you!

Thanks again for the invitation. Sincerely,

Jimmy Bing.

Fran blinked. Jimmy was the man Andre had spent Thanksgiving with. They crewed together when they went to Alaska.

"Brother Joseph? Is there a phone I might use?"

"Of course. It's right here." He moved it forward from behind the counter. Something told Fran that Jimmy was the one person who would know where to find Andre. With her heart pounding out of rhythm, she pressed the buttons and prayed someone was home.

"Hey? Are you Andre Benet?"

Andre stopped in the act of putting things away in his locker. "I am."

"You're wanted dockside."

Andre frowned. "Why? We're almost ready to get under way."

"I have no idea. Somebody told me to tell you."

It was probably Jimmy and his family who'd come to see him off even though he'd told them not to. "Thanks for the message."

"Sure."

There was always a crowd gathered round

during embarkation, especially at a bustling port like San Pedro. Andre disliked the whole miserable scene of families clinging to their loved ones. He generally stayed busy on board until long after the ship had put out to sea.

The last thing he felt like doing right now was going ashore for a final round of good-byes. Jimmy's family had been forced to put up with more than they'd bargained for this time. He'd had no right to inflict his pain on everyone, and had left early for the port in a taxi. Under the circumstances, he didn't know why they'd bothered to come. They didn't deserve more of the same treatment.

Andre supposed he could pretend he hadn't gotten the message. But that would be adding insult to injury. He had to make one last effort at civility before he disappeared. The blackness of a future without Francesca yawned wide before him. He was sinking fast.

''Excuse me,'' he muttered as he slipped past members of the crew settling in. Eventually he found his way to the gangplank and looked around for Jimmy.

Midway down he paused to gaze at the crowd of people shouting to the crewmen on deck. So far he could see no sign of his good friend.

''Andre!''

His head reared back and his eyelids squeezed together. He had to be hallucinating. Out of the many voices, there was one calling his name that sounded too much like Francesca's. Maybe he had gone over the edge. She was in his blood until he couldn't think of anything but her.

''Wait, darling! Don't go! I'm coming!''

Paralyzed with fear that when he opened his eyes it would all be a figment of his imagination, he was slow to react. When he dared to look in the direction of that voice, he could see a woman with shoulder-length gossamer hair desperately attempting to make her way through the throng of people.

The stunning camel-hair coat worn with a long brown-and-white print scarf were unfamiliar. But when she squeezed past another group and looked up, it was Francesca's beautiful face that filled his vision. His heart knocked in his chest.

He couldn't imagine how she would have tracked him here, but right now he didn't care. The only thing of importance was that she'd come all this way to see him. Without conscious thought he started running.

Like all the other seamen over the years who'd literally pushed everyone aside to get to their loved ones waiting on the dock, he found himself doing the same thing. Charged with the energy of ten men, he leaped over the side in an effort to reach her sooner.

The last thing he saw before he caught her in his arms was the glint of liquid green eyes. She felt fantastically warm and vital. He crushed her against his body so they literally swung around.

The way she clung to him as if he were her entire existence was the balm his soul craved. "Thank God I wasn't too late," was all she managed to get out before she broke down completely, uncaring of the people around them.

"Please don't leave me, Andre. Everyone we know and love is painfully aware I want you back. I need you. I love you, my darling."

As her hands lifted to his cheeks, she looked up at him out of a face glistening with tears. "Please say that you forgive me. We'll start all over again. The right way this time. There's so much to tell you, but I can't say it all here.

"Just know that your speech about emotionally crippled sailors made me see myself in a new light. After you left, I went over everything you said to me a hundred times or more.

"I realized that if I couldn't take any risks, then I had allowed my father's behavior to stunt my life. It made me violently angry that he'd already blighted so much of it. That's when I told myself he wasn't going to ruin the rest of it. That's when I drove over to your house, but then I saw that ghastly For Sale sign stuck in the snow. I almost died....

"Oh, Andre—please come back to me," she begged, "and I swear I'll make you the happiest man alive. There is no life without you. I know that now."

Lord. A miracle had happened. He held a Francesca in his arms who had finally opened up her soul to him. The moment was so humbling, he had trouble expressing his thoughts.

"I found my life the day I met you. I've never been the same since," he muttered before his mouth descended.

This time there was a difference in the way she kissed him back. The fear and the striving were gone. In their place was this dizzying sensation of two hearts and bodies merged in total communion.

He was so enthralled by this new side of his passionate darling, he was scarcely aware of the wolf whistles until he heard someone call out, "Hey, Benet— Are you coming with us or not?"

"Not!" he shouted back after he'd put a crimson-faced Francesca at arm's length. "Wait right here, my love, and don't move."

Her eyes shone with a rare luster. "I'm not going anywhere unless it's with you. Oh darling, I'm so in love with you, it hurts." She pressed a hand against her heart.

"I have a remedy for that," he whispered against her lips.

"So do I," she smiled through joyous tears. "Judge Appleby in Elko is waiting to marry us as soon as we can get there. I told him I was ready to make my vows this time. We're booked on a flight out of L.A. airport at three.''

Words weren't sufficient. He crushed her against him once more, then finally whispered, ''Give me five minutes, and I'm all yours.''

''How about the whole of my life.'' The fervency of her tone set a new fire raging in him.

''You're on, my love.''

Nine hours later they stood before Judge Appleby who beamed at them.

''Well, it looks like you went home and counseled together. I told you if your love was meant to be, everything would work out.

''Now repeat after me. I, Francesca Mallory, take this man, Andre Benet, to be my lawfully wedded husband. I solemnly vow to love, honor, and cherish him, to remain faithful to him through sickness or health, through poverty or wealth, through the bad times and the good, until death do us part.''

As Fran said the words in a clear, vibrant voice, she felt Andre's other hand go to the back of her waist and draw her up against him.

The Judge nodded, then told Andre to repeat after him, ''I, Andre Benet, do take this woman, Francesca Mallory to be my lawfully wedded wife. I solemnly vow to love, honor, cherish and protect her, to remain faithful to her through sickness or health, through poverty or wealth, through the bad times and the good, until death do us part.''

Andre's deep voice held a fervency that penetrated to her insides. She bowed her head, brimming with a happiness she'd never experienced before.

''Since you, Francesca, and you, Andre, have vowed before God and this assembly to love each other until death, then by the power invested in me by the court of Elko County, in the State of Nevada of these United States, I hereby proclaim you to be husband and wife.

''What God has joined together, let no man put asunder. You may give her the ring, then kiss your beautiful bride, Mr. Benet.''

Andre let go of her long enough to reach in his suit pocket and draw out the precious ring she'd longed to wear. When he slid it on her finger, it fit perfectly. Before she could countenance it, he pulled her into his strong arms.

''Francesca—'' he cried her name with the same kind of overpowering emotion she was feeling. Compelled by the force of her love, she lifted her eyes, unable to deny him even the smallest secret of her soul.

The answering fire in his dark gaze set off a conflagration as his mouth sought hers with a refined savagery that took the very breath from her body.

Five weeks later, while Fran stood next to her husband to greet their guests in Gerda's living room, she felt Andre's hand slide up her back and caress her neck. "How much longer before we can be alone?" he whispered against her ear, taking advantage of the first lull in the line for the last half hour. It sent shivers of ecstasy through her trembling body.

Every time they came together it was like the first time. Andre had made her feel reborn. The rapture they'd given each other reached levels she didn't know were possible between a man and woman. It had made her thankful to be born a woman. Otherwise she would never know what it was like to be loved by a man like Andre. Just thinking about him, anticipating another night in his bed, in his arms, made it difficult to say a coherent word to anyone.

"I-I'm afraid not for a while. A lot of people from our congregation are still waiting to meet my handsome husband. Do you know, tonight you remind me of the way you looked when I first saw you?" she said a trifle breathlessly.

"If you recall, I was wearing a work shirt and pants I'd borrowed from Brother Joseph. Let's hope this black tux is somewhat of an improvement."

Fran's mouth curved upward. "I wasn't referring to your clothes."

"Really," he teased wickedly.

Her cheeks went hot. "What I meant was, you had a princely bearing. It took my breath, and I haven't caught it since."

She felt the intimate brush of his fingers against her ribcage. "I think I'll wait until later to tell you some of the thoughts running through my mind while I watched your provocative body move in that peach suit you were wearing. I swear you could have tempted the devil himself."

"Andre!"

He kissed her neck. "I love it when you pretend to be shocked."

By now she was enveloped in white-hot heat. Ignoring his comment she said, "If you want to know the truth, I'm the envy of every woman in Gerda's living room."

He shook his dark head. "All eyes are on you, Francesca. Make no mistake about that," he said in a husky aside. "I actually felt sorry for Dr. Barker. The poor devil's still in love with you."

"You're wrong, darling. He would like to be in love the way we are. One day it will happen."

"Maybe. If he's lucky, and meets the right woman. Tonight I feel sorry for anyone who isn't us."

Fran's eyes filled from too much happiness. She knew exactly what he meant. Particularly since she had something earthshaking to tell him.

"Andre—" she whispered tremulously. "After this is over, I'd like to go for a drive."

He flashed her a curious glance. "I must admit I had other plans for us, but I could never say no to you."

"It won't have to take too long."

A strange glint entered his beautiful eyes. ''Do you have a destination in mind?''

''Yes.''

''Is this some sort of surprise?''

She flashed him a provocative smile. ''You'll have to wait to find out.''

''You shouldn't have told me that,'' he half growled. ''Now I can't wait to leave.''

''If you did that you would disappointment everyone, particularly Gerda and Mother who've practically killed themselves to make this party perfect for us.''

''In that case, I'll be good. As it happens, they're both favorites of mine.''

Two hours later Andre finally got his wife to himself. ''Where did you want to drive?'' Curiosity had been eating him alive.

''Just continue south on the freeway until I tell you to turn off.''

She was behaving so mysteriously, Andre didn't know what to think. Evidently there were things still to be revealed after five weeks of marriage. But he wasn't complaining. On the contrary, life with Francesca had surpassed his conception of wedded bliss.

"Take the next exit, darling."

"Whatever you say," he murmured, feasting his eyes on her lovely profile. Tonight she radiated a beauty that made her glow. In fact he was so entranced by his wife in this mood, it didn't register that they were on the road to the monastery until she told him to drive through the gates.

Whatever surprise he'd thought might be waiting for him at the end of their little journey, he would never have imagined her wanting to come here. It was close to midnight and freezing out.

"Francesca?"

"In a few minutes your questions will be answered. If it's all right with you, I'd like us to visit your father's grave."

He blinked in astonishment, but as she seemed set on it, he levered himself from the car and went around the passenger side to help her out.

"It's too cold here for you."

"I'm fine with your arm around me."

A half moon made the grounds a little lighter than the last time he'd come to say goodbye. That seemed a lifetime ago when he was another man.

By tacit agreement their footsteps slowed as they approached the spot where he'd watched the brothers bury his father last spring.

Slowly she turned to him and put her hands on his arms. "Andre, my love— I have something to tell you that I thought your father would like to hear if he's listening."

Andre's heart started to thud.

A smile illuminated her face. "We're going to have a baby, darling. I just found out yesterday, and the news has left me overjoyed.

"It seemed right to come here, because this is the place where everything happened, where we both fell in love. And all because Abbot Ambrose, your father, had agreed to do a story for the magazine.

"I-I used to think things happened by accident. But looking back to last April, I'm now convinced that when your aunt told you about your father, and when I was sent out here in Paul's place, it was destiny. *Our* destiny. And now it's our baby's."

Andre couldn't think, couldn't speak. All he could do was gather his beloved in his arms. This beautiful, wonderful woman whose body held their future, had just made the circle of his life complete.

MILLS & BOON® PUBLISH EIGHT LARGE PRINT TITLES A MONTH. THESE ARE THE EIGHT TITLES FOR MARCH 2000

MARRIAGE ULTIMATUM
Lindsay Armstrong

MISTRESS BY ARRANGEMENT
Helen Bianchin

BARTALDI'S BRIDE
Sara Craven

TO TAME A BRIDE
Susan Fox

THE SICILIAN'S MISTRESS
Lynne Graham

BRIDEGROOM ON APPROVAL
Day Leclaire

SLADE BARON'S BRIDE
Sandra Marton

HUSBAND POTENTIAL
Rebecca Winters

MILLS & BOON® PUBLISH EIGHT LARGE PRINT TITLES A MONTH. THESE ARE THE EIGHT TITLES FOR APRIL 2000

A MARRIAGE BETRAYED
Emma Darcy

AN ENGAGEMENT OF CONVENIENCE
Catherine George

LONG-LOST BRIDE
Day Leclaire

MORGAN'S CHILD
Anne Mather

A YULETIDE SEDUCTION
Carole Mortimer

THE BACHELOR'S BARGAIN
Jessica Steele

CLAIMING HIS CHILD
Margaret Way

DESERT HONEYMOON
Anne Weale